Woof Woof Story

I TOLD YOU TO TURN ME INTO A
Pampered Pooch,
NOT FENRIR!

Inumajin

ILLUSTRATION BY
Kochimo

Routa

He should have been freed from a life of labor and gotten reincarnated as a dog, but no matter how you look at him, he's clearly growing into a wolf. Now he has to try his best to act as doglike as possible, because if his true identity is revealed...

Zenobia

A freeloading knight currently crashing at the mansion. She doesn't buy Routa's dog act for a second.

Mary

Routa's owner and the daughter of an incredibly wealthy family. She's a kind, proper young lady who spoils Routa rotten.

Hecate

A mysterious forest witch. She's well versed in medicine and trusted by all.

Contents

PROLOGUE · · · 001

01 I'm a Pet Just Like I Wanted!
    ...Or So I Thought, but I'm Actually a Ferocious Beast! ··· 005

02 A Ferocious Beast!
    ...Or So I Thought, but I Apologize for Nothing! ··· 017

03 A Ferocious Beast!
    ...Or So I Thought, but I'm Actually a Magical Beast! ··· 037

04 An Encounter with Magical Dogs and Cats!
    ...Or So I Thought, but It Was Actually a High-Calorie Lunch! ··· 061

05 A *Yuri* Scene?!
    ...Or So I Thought, but Instead, There Was a Mysterious Illness! ··· 095

06 I'm Just Going to Get a Plant!
    ...Or So I Thought, but It Was Actually an Adventure! ··· 119

07 No Escape!
    ...Or So I Thought, but It Was Actually a Nice Creature! ··· 139

~BONUS EPISODE~

EX What a Kind Goddess!
    ...Or So I Thought, but She Was Actually Useless! ··· 161

AFTERWORD · · · 171

Woof Woof Story

I TOLD YOU TO TURN ME INTO A Pampered Pooch, NOT FENRIR!

1

Inumajin

ILLUSTRATION BY

Kochimo

YEN ON

NEW YORK

Woof Woof Story

I TOLD YOU TO TURN ME INTO A *Pampered Pooch,* NOT FENRIR!

VOLUME 1

Inumajin

Translation by Jennifer O'Donnell
Cover art by Kochimo

WANWAN MONOGATARI Volume 1 -KANEMOCHI NO INU NI SHITETOWA ITTAGA, FENRIR NISHIROTOWA ITTENEE!-
Copyright © Inumajin, Kochimo 2017
First published in Japan in 2017 by KADOKAWA CORPORATION, Tokyo.
English translation rights arranged with KADOKAWA CORPORATION, Tokyo,
through TUTTLE-MORI AGENCY, INC., Tokyo.

English translation © 2019 by Yen Press, LLC

Yen On
1290 Avenue of the Americas
New York, NY 10104

Visit us at yenpress.com

facebook.com/yenpress
twitter.com/yenpress

yenpress.tumblr.com
instagram.com/yenpress

First Yen On Edition: February 2019

Yen On is an imprint of Yen Press, LLC.
The Yen On name and logo are trademarks of Yen Press, LLC.

Library of Congress Cataloging-in-Publication Data
Names: Inumajin, author. | Kochimo, illustrator. | O'Donnell, Jennifer, translator.
Title: Woof woof story : I told you to turn me into a pampered pooch, not fenrir! / Inumajin ;
illustration by Kochimo ; translation by Jennifer O'Donnell ; cover art by Kochimo.
Other titles: Wanwan Monogatari. English | I told you to turn me into a pampered pooch, not fenrir!
Description: First Yen On edition. | New York, NY : Yen On, 2018–
Identifiers: LCCN 2018051028 | ISBN 9781975303181 (v. 1 : pbk.)
Subjects: CYAC: Reincarnation—Fiction. | Wishes—Fiction. | Dogs—Fiction. | Fantasy.
Classification: LCC PZ7.1.I63 Wo 2018 | DDC [Fic]—dc23
LC record available at https://lccn.loc.gov/2018051028

ISBNs: 978-1-9753-0318-1 (paperback)
978-1-9753-0319-8 (ebook)

1 3 5 7 9 10 8 6 4 2

LSC-C

Printed in the United States of America

Prologue

"Ah, so this is death."

I murmur to myself as the world grows dim.

The cause of death is a no-brainer. Overwork.

I haven't slept in forever. I haven't been home in who knows how long. What day is it even?

My body, completely exhausted after being worked to the bone, loses what little strength it has left and crumples forward like a puppet cut from its strings.

I can't even muster the strength to catch myself.

All I can do is obey the laws of gravity and go hurtling toward the hard ground.

My first kiss is going to be with my company building's floor. What a pathetic way to go out.

Ah... I wish I'd stuffed myself and had a good night's sleep before dying... If I get reincarnated, just bring me back as the pet dog of some wealthy family...

One last crazy wish flutters across my fading consciousness.

The dead eyes of my colleagues are all focused on their own work. None of them even noticed I've collapsed.

Even if they did, they just keep on working.

Unusual incidents aren't even recognized as unusual. That's corporate hell for you.

They're all completely brainwashed. Here I am, a fellow employee, dropping dead right next to them, and they don't even flinch.

I'm pretty sure my death, and the toxic work environment that caused it, will get swept under the rug by my smooth-talking superiors.

You're all horrible. At least I get to be the first one to retire.

I bid my ghastly coworkers a silent farewell.

This is how it ends, yet I don't feel a tinge of regret.

Just the feeling of peaceful release.

Suddenly, my face hits the ground.

Life as a pet doesn't sound so bad, actually...

I surrender my soul to the abyss.

"YOUR WISH SHALL BE GRANTED!!"

"Arww, arww... *(So warm...)*"

It feels like I fell asleep in something soft.

Did someone wrap me in a blanket and put me on this futon? It's hard to move.

I'm still so drowsy that it's hard to wake up completely.

"Arwarw... *(What happened? Er... I kissed the floor, died, then......)*"

I feel like I heard a woman's voice the moment I died.

I faintly recall talking to her, and I think she agreed to something or other, but my memory's a total blur.

Okay, let's backtrack. First off, who am I?

"Arww, arwarw... *(My name is Routa Okami. Twenty-nine-year-old office worker. No hobbies. No friends. No girlfriend. No family. No wife. Just a long list of "nos." I guess "noice" guys really do finish last.)*"

Aaaand now I'm bummed out.

Come to think of it, I can't recall a single good thing ever happening to me. I led an extremely average life, trudged through a bleak existence as a corporate slave, and then died from overwork.

Oh, right. I did die, didn't I? So why do I feel so alive? What's going on? Where the heck am—?

"Oh, he's awake! He's awake, Father!"

"Arw...? *(Huh...?)*"

I look up in search of the voice and am greeted by a pair of large, round blue eyes.

"Arw?! *(A-a giant...?!)*"

A pair of enormous hands reach down and pick me up.

"Arw! Arw! *(Hey! Whoa! Stop it!)*"

Geez, that *arw, arw* sound is really getting on my nerves! What is it?! I'm currently freaking out, and that really isn't helping! Enough with the cutesy voice already!

"Arf! Arf!"

I can only hear the high-pitched yelp when I try to say something.

"...Arw......?! *(...N-no way...?! Is that* my *voice...?!)*"

It sounds like a puppy's.

Wait, a puppy?

...Oh, right. It's all coming back to me now. I guess I did wish for something like this just before I died. Then I heard a woman saying she'd grant me my wish.

"Arww...?! *(Did I really get reincarnated...?!)*"

Any lingering traces of doubt are snuffed out in an instant.

Reflected in the windowpane of a nearby cabinet is a young blue-eyed girl. Cradled against her chest is something undeniably canine, an adorable puppy covered in white fur with short legs on a fluffy body, a perfectly round puffball.

There's no denying it. I've been reincarnated as a dog.

"So cute! You're just the cutest! Oh, Father, I want this one!"

"Hmm, very well, then. Make sure you take good care of him. But I must say, you're rarely this persistent about anything, Mary."

The man standing behind the girl nods.

He's a tall, regal, attractive gentleman. I can't help but feel a little jealous.

"Shop assistant! We'll take this one."

I wonder if he's the girl's dad. He calls out to a man in an apron who fits the description of "shop assistant."

"Of course. At once, sir... Hmm? Did we have a dog like this?"

The shop assistant adjusts his round glasses while staring right at me.

"His pedigree does not concern me. If this is the dog my daughter wants, then it is the one she shall have."

The father interjects as he strokes his magnificent beard.

"O-of course, sir. I will make the necessary preparations immediately. The young lady will need a carrier."

"No I won't. I'll bring him home like this!"

The girl holds me up above her head and twirls around. Her blond hair glitters in contrast to her plain-colored skirt as she spins.

Whoa, whoa, don't I get a say in this?

"Oh, right, I need to give you a name!"

At first glance, she looks like a strict young lady, but her smile shines like the sun. She is incredibly cute. Her eyes are more beautiful than those foreign celebrities. As she squeezes me, I'm consumed by her warmth. I nuzzle my face into her and get engulfed by the smell of flowers.

"Arw! *(Okay, I've decided! Your home'll do!)*"

You can pet me as much as you like. And in return, take good care of me.

Feed me amazing food! Spoil me rotten!

All I've done is suffer until now. From this day forward, I'm not going to work at all! I'm going to live my life doing nothing and eat ridiculous amounts of food.

The pet life I've only ever dreamed about starts now!

† † †

"Grwl, grwl! *(Meat is so good! Meat is so good!)*"

I rip flesh from bone as I enjoy a steak so rare that it's still dripping with blood. How can they afford to feed a dog this well? These people have way too much money. Maybe the reason I can never seem to eat enough is because the food here is just so tasty.

More. I need more meat! Give me meat!

"Honestly. Please eat more calmly, Routa."

The young lady who took me home smiles in amazement. Her hand gently stroking my back feels incredible.

My pet name is the same one I had in my previous life: Routa. It's a crazy coincidence, but it turns out that Routa was the name of some famous hero who saved this world. Lady Mary loves to read, and she chose it from one of her favorite hero stories.

Way to go, Other World Routa. I mean, it's not like I've ever saved the world or anything, and I won't be doing so anytime soon. Deeds of heroism just aren't in the cards for me. I'm happy living the pampered pooch life until the day I die.

"Grwl, grwl! *(Oh my God, this meat is so good!)*"

Time has really flown by since the day Lady Mary picked me up. Well, I say that, but it's only been a month.

As a puppy, I had a milk-based diet, but that was only for the first week. It wasn't long before I didn't need milk anymore and started devouring two kilos of meat per day.

"This dog sure can eat."

The old chef who prepares my meat watches me with wide eyes.

On the menu today, we have a sautéed veal dish. It's made with the leftovers from the family's crown roast, but they don't mind at all. They're incredibly kind and won't feed me any old slice of raw meat just because I'm a dog. The meals don't have very complex flavors, but I haven't cared at all since I was reincarnated. In fact, I can't get enough of the deliciousness of meat. These days, I couldn't care less about flavoring or refinement. Grilling it like this is more than enough. Excellent work, old man!

"That's fine; I think it's cute. Eat lots and grow really big, Routa."

"Grwl!"

I growl in response and rub my cheek against hers. I hold back from licking her face so that she doesn't get covered in drool. Play it cool. Who's a good boy? That's right. Me.

"Ha-ha."

She blissfully closes her sky-blue eyes as she pets my head.

Her full name is Meariya Von Faulks.

She was born in this palatial mansion as the daughter of a noble family. She's the only daughter of the prestigious merchant Gandolf Von Faulks and now my owner. This guardian goddess of my cushy pet life turns fourteen this year. The master of little old me. I pray I get to live a long life with her. Especially one where I don't have to work.

"Huh? What's wrong? Does your tummy hurt? Shall I give it a scratch?"

I show her my belly, and she gently scratches it with her slender fingertips. Utter bliss.

"Haff-haff-haff-haff! *(Ah yeah, right there, that's the spot!)*"

"Well, that's a dirty old man face if ever I've seen one."

The old chef looks at me writhing on the floor and raises an eyebrow in surprise.

"He is not an old man! He's a very cute boy. Right here? Does this feel good?"

"Haff-haff-haff! *(Ohhh, this is the best!)*"

I have attained nirvana. There isn't a dog alive who's as happy as the dog of a rich family. Truly heaven on earth. That's the kind of life I want to live. Oh, wait—I already am! May the good times last forever!

† † †

One lazy day in the mansion's great hall, I find myself cozied up for a nap.

"Master, something is not right about that dog," a shrill voice rings out.

Looking up, I see two humans ascending the grand stairway. Lady Mary's father, Gandolf, is followed closely by a sword-wielding woman. It's the middle of the day, yet she's wearing armor, looking ready to leap into battle at any moment. Her fiery red hair is tied into a ponytail, and she's wearing a harsh, critical expression.

She's a knight who sponges off the family and crashes here in the mansion. I'm pretty sure her name was something super-tough sounding, like Zenobia Lionheart.

"Grwwl…? *(You got something to say…?)*"

I foggily look up at them as I sprawl out in the hall at the bottom of the stairs.

"Hmm. What do you mean something isn't right about Routa? He looks like an ordinary dog to me."

"In what way?! He's only been here a month! Just a month!! Don't you think it's strange that he's already this big?? Dogs don't get this big this fast! He might be the spawn of some mountain wolf. We need to dispose of him before it's too late!"

Gandolf puts up his hand to stop her, then points to me.

"What are you saying, Zenobia? This dog is my daughter's greatest treasure. Getting rid of him would break her heart."

He's right. How could you say you want to dispose of me? Don't you know how much Lady Mary relies on me? We're together from the moment we wake up to the moment we fall asleep after a bath. I've got time to kill because right now she's studying with the family tutor, but besides that, we're inseparable.

"Forget about hurting her feelings, what about her well-being?! Just look at him! She couldn't possibly be safe around a beast like that. He's clearly planning to attack the moment we let our guard down! Just leave it to me! I'll finish him off with one fell swoop!"

Whoa, whoa! This knight's saying some rude things.

"I have a responsibility to protect the people of this household!"

"I invited you here as our guest. You need not take on that much responsibility. I am truly grateful that you think of our family that way, though."

The venerable Papa Gandolf flashes her a beaming smile.

"Then…!"

"But I'm still against it. Just look at that lazy lump. Does he really look like that much of a violent beast to you?"

"Grrrwl… *(Sleepy, sleepy…)*"

I let out a massive yawn and scratch my ear with my back leg.

No matter how you look at me, I'm just a harmless hound, Zenobia. I'm not a beast at all, just an overgrown puppy. C'mon, how about a pet?

"Tch... Please excuse me!"

It seems we weren't able to change her mind, so Zenobia, the freeloading knight, storms off grumbling.

"Ugh!"

"Grwl! *(Eek...!)*"

The death glare she gives me as she passes is terrifying. Why is she so mean to a li'l puppy like me? How horrible...

"My, oh my. She's got a lot going for her, but that stiff personality of hers is a bit of a fly in the ointment, eh, Routa?"

Yep. I think so, too, Papa.

I'm not a beast; I'm not even a guard dog.

I'm just a slacker...

Oh! Right there! Scratch right under the neck...

† † †

"Hmm. ♪ Hmmm. ♪"

Lady Mary is humming a cheery tune as she chooses her outfit for the day. The sight of her standing there in just her underwear is a little risqué, but since I'm a dog, I don't care. Well, my soul is human, so I would be lying if I said I was completely unfazed. But even I wouldn't lay a paw on such a beauty. I'm a firm believer in "look but don't touch."

But it doesn't count if Lady Mary is the one touching me.

"How about this one, miss?"

The maid standing next to her shows her a dress.

"It is a splendid indigo, but don't you think it's a little restricting?"

"We are only heading out to the lake. Does matter if the dress is restrictive?"

"Why, yes. I won't be able to play with Routa if it's too tight. Right, Routa? What do you think of this dress?"

"Grwl! *(You're the cutest in the whole world, Lady Mary! It doesn't matter what you wear, you'll still be the cutest! We can just enjoy our lunch beneath the shade of the trees and laze around!)*"

"Really? Well, if you say so, I'll wear this one, then."

"Oh, can you understand what Routa is saying, miss?"

"Of course. It's Routa, after all!"

"My goodness." The maid chuckles.

I get caught up in the friendly atmosphere and wag my tail.

Wag, wag.

"Grwl. *(Oh, whoops.)*"

My tail catches on the laundry basket and tosses the clothes Lady Mary had just taken off everywhere.

I'm still getting used to my rapidly growing dog body. These things happen from time to time.

I begin looking for the clothes that scattered everywhere, including near a full-length mirror.

"Oh, do be careful, Routa!"

"Grwl, grwl. *(Whoops, sorry. Don't worry, though, Miss Maid.)*"

I quickly move to pick up the dirty laundry. A regular family dog wouldn't think to do something like this. And of course, I'm not about to pick it up with my mouth. They would get all sticky with drool. So I use my tail to scoop them up and put them back in the basket.

"Wow, what a clever boy you are, Routa!"

"Grwl. *(Right? Even I'm willing to work sometimes.)*"

It isn't long before I'm tail-tossing the clothes into the basket like a pro.

"Grwl...? *(Hmm...?)*"

Then suddenly, I spot it.

Something strangely disturbing is reflected in the large mirror Lady Mary uses to get dressed.

It's me. But something seems off.

Now that I think about it, I haven't been able to get a good look at myself since the day I was bought. It only takes a momentary glance to see that I'm actually a pretty good-looking dog. Once Lady Mary starts getting changed and isn't occupying the mirror, I sit in front of it to get a better look.

I look from the front, the side, and all directions to make sure that I am indeed looking at my own face.

"G-grwl...! *(H-hang on a sec...! I look amazing!)*"

I swoon at my own beauty.

My white fur is incredibly fluffy and soft, no doubt thanks to my daily baths. My large ears are pointed and so sharp they wouldn't miss a sound no matter how far away it was. My eyes are long slits, and my emerald irises shine with a cold gleam.

"...Grwl? *(...Huh?)*"

My large mouth is lined with teeth so sharp they could kill with a single bite. My body is so burly it doesn't even come close to the average dog. And my legs are so slender and toned that they could probably run like the wind, even carrying this huge body.

"...Grwl, grwl? *(...Huh? Huh?)*"

What sharp eyes I have... What strong legs I have... What big teeth I have...

The body is much too big to be a dog's, and the face is just a little too wild...

"Grwl... *(...Am I really a dog?)*"

No. Thinking realistically, there can't possibly be a breed of dog with a face this ferocious. If a neighborhood family got a dog that looked like this, they would be reported right away.

Why do you guys seem so calm about this?!

This is not something to be taken lightly!

No matter how you look at it, I'm not a dog. I'm a wolf!

I take another look in the mirror. As I push my nose right up against the glass, I'm even more taken aback.

"Grwl...! *(Yikes. Just look at that face. What the hell? I'm way too*

*intimidating…! I'd pee myself if I encountered something like this…!
No, I'd probably poop myself, too…!)*"

I understand exactly what that knight Zenobia was talking about
now. It's dangerous to keep a beast like this around the house.

Come to think of it, a dog wouldn't have such a terrifying growl.
There's nothing pet-like about this sound whatsoever. It's all beast.

If I managed to get this big in only one month, I can't imagine
how big I'll be after a whole year. If I get any bigger, Papa will definitely get rid of me.

"Grw… *(Th-this is bad…)*"

Dangerous animals are exterminated. That's just common sense
no matter what world you live in.

The terrifying image of Zenobia brandishing her blade crosses
my mind.

"Grr…? Grwl…? *(Wh-what do I do…? What do I do…?)*"

I-I'm going to die.

I'm going to be abandoned to live the life of a wild dog.

I just want to spend my days carefree, eating and sleeping!

I don't know what to do.

My life as a dog—no, as a wolf—has taken a pretty dramatic
turn, and I'm seriously worried for the first time ever. I don't think
I've ever been this worried before, even as a human.

"Grr…! *(Okay, then…!)*"

I just need to calm down and think. I can find a solution to this.

"What's wrong, Routa? You look upset. Does your tummy hurt?"

Lady Mary gives me a worried expression. She looks so cute tucking her long blond hair behind her ear.

I've made up my mind, Lady Mary. I'll do whatever it takes to
preserve this new life I've been given.

I—! I—!

I look up at my lady—

"…Grrf. Arf! Arf!"

—and resolve to keep up the dog act like my life depends on it.

The image of a great white wolf is reflected on the surface of the lake.

I stare back at it, feeling depressed.

"Grwl... *(No doubt about it. No matter how you look at me, I'm not a dog, I'm a wolf. It's a miracle I haven't already been discovered... Everyone besides that knight must be blind.)*"

I sigh deeply.

Everyone's going to think it's strange if I grow any larger. And the more I look at it, the more terrifying this face is.

"Routa!"

The water splashes at my lady's call, and the image of the wolf vanishes in the waves.

"The water's cold, and it feels great. Come swim with me."

The edges of her skirt are drawn up in true tomboy fashion as she rushes over to me. She looks like a water fairy playing in the shallows of the lake.

"Grr... A-arf! *(C-coming!)*"

That was close.

I almost replied normally and let my feral growl slip out.

I'm a dog.

I'm a dog.

I'm a harmless, incompetent puppy dog.

All right! Self-motivation complete.

"Come on. You're not scared of the water, are you? You love baths so much."

Lady Mary grabs hold of my front two legs and pulls as hard as she can, but my body is so huge, I don't budge at all.

"W-woof, woof! *(I-I'm coming, my lady!)*"

I consciously make my voice higher, trying to mimic a dog's bark. This is harder than I thought. I'm gonna need to practice.

"Come on! It's not scary at all."

"Arrf, arrf."

I try as hard as I can to sound like a dog, and I play in the water with her.

† † †

Shake, shake, shake.

I shake with all my might, flinging water everywhere.

"Eek!"

Water sprays over Lady Mary, and she laughs.

My white fur returns to its once fluffy state now that I've shaken out all the water.

"Ha-ha, look at that, Routa. You made a rainbow."

The mist made from the spraying water reflects the brilliant rays of sunlight, creating the arch of a rainbow. The beautiful scene is only there for a moment as the heat of early summer evaporates the mist and the rainbow along with it.

"Hey, Routa?"

My lady looks at me eagerly.

"Arf? *(Ohhh, you want to see it again? All right, then.)*"

I'm about to jump from the shore into the lake when the maid, who was sitting in the carriage, calls out to us.

"Lady Mary! It's time to head back. You still have your afternoon classes."

Oh, looks like lunchtime's over. No surprise considering how long it takes to get back to the mansion.

"Aw, that's a shame. Let's go, Routa. We can't keep the teacher waiting."

"Woof, woof! *(It must be exhausting studying from morning to night, my lady. I'll eat and sleep extra for you! Just leave it to me!)*"

We head back to the carriage as I console her.

The carriage could easily fit four people, but half the seats are for me. It hadn't occurred to me before, but I take up a lot of space. And I feel like I'm still growing. I try to make myself as small as possible in the seat.

"Let us be off, then."

The volunteer driver for the day is none other than the freeloading knight, Zenobia.

"Tch. Tch."

As she flicks the reins and clicks her tongue, the two horses start slowly in the direction of home, pulling the carriage behind them. They gradually pick up speed until the wind comes blowing in.

This is the perfect time to explain the new world I was reincarnated into.

First, imagine medieval Europe.

Rows of buildings with stone architecture. Golden fields of wheat. The sound of woodcutters' axes echoing out of the deep forest.

It's as beautiful as a folk song.

But then, there are things mixed in that stand out from the norm, things like swords and sorcery. Creatures known as monsters also seem common in this world, and part-time workers known as adventurers go out on a daily basis to fight them.

The knight sitting in the driver's seat is one of them.

She's crashing at the Faulkses' mansion for now, but apparently, Zenobia used to do some adventuring of her own. It seems that fighting monsters was her forte. Her battle prowess doesn't do her much good these days, however. She doesn't have anyone to fight.

This area is actually supposed to be pretty unique, since monsters don't approach it thanks to the sacred lake.

Which means that Zenobia, the knight with nothing to fight, has as little work as I do. The extent of her usefulness has been reduced to tagging along whenever Papa or Lady Mary leave the house.

She's a good-for-nothing just like me! HA-HA-HA!

...I just realized something. That would make her my rival!

This house isn't big enough for two deadbeats! Well, it is, but it isn't!

For the sake of my own cushy lifestyle, I need to come up with a way to defeat Zenobia...

No need to rush, though. Let's get back to the story.

The sunlight glitters in my eyes, reflecting off the giant lake outside the carriage.

It's been said that a giant crystal sank to the bottom of the lake, granting it the sacred properties that keep the monsters away.

You'd think it would be frowned upon for my lady and me to play around in such a sacred lake, but all the land surrounding the mansion, for as far as the eye can see, belongs to Papa. No one gets angry with us. This family must be loaded to own acres upon acres of land that's mostly monster-free forest.

Score! This pup definitely hit the jackpot. I just need to do something about the knight...!

With these lands safe from just about any monster threat, Zenobia, the only armed person for miles, takes it upon herself to keep a watchful eye on me. She even volunteered to be the carriage driver just so she could make sure I didn't get up to anything.

Then again, I understand how she feels. I'd be on my guard, too, if I were her. There's no telling when a massive wolf, such as myself, might attack Lady Mary.

I had a feeling she wouldn't let me ride in the carriage on the way back, but if she'd tried that, I would've just used my natural homing instincts to find my way back.

You won't get rid of me that easily! Never! I'm like a parasite that refuses to die! Don't underestimate how attached a human who died from overwork can be to a life of loafing!

I huff, cementing my resolution to my pet life.

† † †

The two-horse carriage proceeds down the dirt road through the forest.

The lake isn't that far from the mansion. After thirty-something minutes of rattling, the estate comes into view.

"Haff-haff-haff-haff. *(Phew, it sure is stuffy in this carriage.)*"

I stick my head out the carriage window, letting my tongue loll.

It's early summer, but the wind is still cold. I lift my nose, enjoying the forest smell in the air way more than I thought I would.

"Arf...? *(Hmm?)*"

There's an odd smell mixed in with the scent of greenery. It's incredibly faint, but it's a stench I've never smelled before.

I try to zero in on the scent again and sniff around a bit more.

Hmm, this is a worrying smell. I have a bad feeling about it. Where? Where is it coming from?

Sniff, sniff, sniff. Ah. *Sniff, sniff, sniff.*

"...Hey, mutt. What are you up to?" Zenobia's voice snaps from the driver's seat.

I look up to see the knight's horrific expression.

"Arw?! *(Eek?!)*"

Our driver is looking my way with murderous intent in her eyes. Zenobia's death glare is trained right on me...! Scary!

What?! What did I do wrong?! I just want to live a life that doesn't require me to do anything, a pet life where everything is taken care of for me!

"What's wrong, Routa? Is there a bug or something?"

"Arww! *(That's not it at all, my lady! This knight is bullying me! Tell her off!)*"

"Oh, the back of your ear itches? Right here?"

"Arw, arw! *(That's not it, either, my lady! I should be the only good-for-nothing in this household! Get rid of her! Get rid of this terrifying woman right now!)*"

"Is it your tummy? Under your armpits?"

"Arww, arww! *(Ah. This is when my meaning doesn't reach you?! Ah, that's not it at all! Oh! Right there! Aw yeeeaaah! That feels so gooooooood!)*"

While scratching me, Lady Mary hits a spot that feels especially good, and I can't resist any longer. She pets me for the entire thirty-minute carriage ride back to the mansion.

† † †

We climb out of the horse-drawn carriage once it arrives at its destination.

"All right then, I'm off for my studies, so wait for me! We'll have dinner once I'm done and then a bath!"

"Woof, woof! *(Very well, my lady! I'll enjoy a nap while I wait for you!)*"

Hey! That bark just now was pretty doglike, wasn't it?

I happily wag my tail in response to Lady Mary. She waves back at me as she heads into the mansion with the maid.

"…Hey."

I hear a threatening voice behind me. The sudden, intense murderous aura I feel sends a chill up my spine. It's Zenobia, of course.

Crap. I really don't want to turn around.

"There's something I need to talk to you about once I've taken the carriage back. Wait here."

Her eyes are blazing as she leads the horses away.

Wh-what could she have to say to me?

I'm scared.

What's she going to do?!

What's she going to do to me?!

† † †

"Ohhm, ohhm! *(Bone crackers are so good! They're just fried-up bones, but they're still so good!)*"

In just a few minutes, I'm already eating the snacks the old chef had given me—crackers made from calf bones dried in the heat of the sun, then slowly fried in oil. The old chef had done a splendid job. A soul who doesn't waste a single ingredient is truly wonderful.

The crushed bones let out a juice brimming with umami, which matches the crunchy texture perfectly, truly making it a jewelry box of flavors!

"Whoa, slow down a little when you eat. You sure can put it away, huh?"

The old chef watches me stuff myself with a startled look on his face, but he also seems happy to see me greedily scarf down the food.

"Woof, woof! *(These are so absolutely amazing, old man! Thanks!)*"

"...I feel like you've suddenly started barking more like a dog... Oh wait, you were always a dog.

"Bwa-ha-ha!" the old man laughs as he ruffles my head.

The way you pet me isn't half-bad. Pet me more. And keep thinking I'm a dog.

"Awwwn. *(Now that my tummy is nice and full, I think I'm going to treat myself to a nap right here with the old man.)*"

I curl up in the corner of the room so I don't get in the way, tucking my luxurious tail under my head to use as a pillow.

"Grwl... *(Good night...)*"

The sound of the chef's knife chopping away in preparation for the evening's meal makes me feel good, and drowsiness takes over.

I'm on the verge of falling asleep when—

"Y-you liiiiittle—!! So this is where you weeere!!"

Just as I hear a clatter and a crash, the knight bursts into the kitchen.

"Why didn't you waaaait?! I told you we had to taaaalk!!"

Wh-whoa?! If it isn't Zenobia. What's wrong? What's gotten you so riled up?

The old chef is so shocked, he extinguishes the fire on the stove and turns around.

Zenobia, who was looking at me, shifts her focus and quickly tries to fix her appearance.

"Oh, I-I'm terribly sorry, Lord James."

"Would you like some snacks, too, Zenobia? I'm sorry to say these are all I have, but……"

He takes the plate with the leftover bone crackers, sprinkles them with some rock salt, and hands them to her.

"N-no, that's not why... My thanks. I'll have just one."

She takes a stick-shaped rib, scrunches up her shoulder a little to conceal her eating, and nibbles on it.

I'm surprised at the amount of grace contained in the gesture. And how cute it makes her.

Once she finishes her snack, she bows her head.

"It was a wonderful treat. You have my thanks."

When she looks up again, her gaze returns to me.

"…Come."

Just as I realize she's walking toward me, she grabs the scruff of my neck and yanks.

"Arww, arww! *(Ah, n-no, stop it! You're being too rough! I've seen how this plays out in fan fiction! …Tch. I'll get you!)*"

"Tch, I'll get you!" —I actually said that.

I would much rather switch positions with Zenobia. I'd like to see her chained up, saying "Tch. I'll get you."

My resistance is futile as she drags me through the back door and outside.

† † †

Zenobia and I square off against each other in a secluded park of the garden.

"The young lady isn't here. I know you're not really a dog. Show me your true form. You cannot trick me."

"Arww."

"A dog could never grow this huge in just a month. And look at your face. You're clearly a wolf. First, the master gets won over, and now everyone else is on board. Why doesn't anyone in this mansion find this strange?"

"Arw?"

"...Do not think ill of me. I must dispose of you before you remember your wild nature. It will be too late if you attack the lady."

"Arww, arww."

"I-it's pointless! I shall not falter even if you use such a pitiful voice!"

Zenobia draws her sword as she shouts.

Tch. My plan to appeal to her emotions failed. I didn't think anyone could resist my cuteness. Not bad, Zenobia.

No, wait—this isn't the time to be praising her.

She's serious. Dead serious.

This lady's really out for blood!

"Before you do any harm, I, Zenobia Lionheart, shall cut you down!"

Following this declaration, she raises her sword high above her head.

"Arf?! *(Wha—?! No way?!)*"

Seriously?! Can't we settle this some other way?!

I thought there'd be a bit more buildup! This is all happening so fast, I didn't have time to get ready!

W-wait! Hold on! I'm gonna die! I'm really gonna die!

I don't even have time to think about dodging it.

With terrifying speed, the sword slashes down.

The blade strikes my head cleanly, and the force behind the attack instantly splits it in half.

...The sword, that is.

It lets out a metallic screech, and the broken end tumbles through the air.

"...Arw? *(...Huh?)*"

"Th-th-that's impossible..."

Zenobia stands before me, flustered.

I survey my body while trying to make sense of what just happened. Surprisingly, there isn't a single drop of blood.

Amazing! I'm unharmed! I'm alive! Thank God!

Actually, if I hadn't been reincarnated as a wolf in the first place, this would have never happened. I'm not thankful at all!

"I-it can't be... My sword... A sword forged by the craftsman Rouen...," she mumbles as she falls to her knees.

She remains crumpled there as she stares dumbfounded at the broken sword.

...Ohhh. I see.

Dear, sweet Zenobia, it seems you've been swindled. That sword is a fake.

You poor thing.

It's clearly just some crummy old sword that someone sold to you for a fortune under the pretense that it was a rare artifact.

"That...can't be... I spent so much money on it..."

Called it. That was painfully predictable.

Zenobia looks so sad that I can't help but call out to her.

"Arww... *(Um...)*"

"You...!"

Eek! She's glaring at me.

Ah. Upon closer inspection, her eyes are welling up with tears.

She's gonna cry.

The knight's sword broke, and now she's about to cry.

"Y-you! You're no ordinary wolf!"

"Woof, woof. *(Nope. I'm an ordinary dog.)*"

"Shut up! It's useless to keep pretending you're a dog! ...I will not let this farce continue! You'd best prepare yourself for next time!"

She delivers a parting shot and runs away.

She's so unreasonable.

First, she attacks me; then, she starts sobbing and insulting me.

But I guess getting to see Zenobia flustered was a reward in its own right. I'm definitely grateful for that.

Maybe I'll try to cheer her up with some face licks.

† † †

"What's that? Zenobia isn't here today?"

The maid nods in reply to Lady Mary.

"Yes. She told me she was going to the city to purchase a new sword. It appears she won't return to the mansion for a while."

"Really? I was hoping I could go to the lake with Routa again today..."

Lady Mary, who was excited to go out and play now that her afternoon classes had finished, droops her shoulders dejectedly.

Oh, right. Her sword broke the other day. Is an unarmed knight even a knight? It sounds like Zenobia's gone on a journey to retrieve her identity. You could say that I was the one responsible for shattering that identity in the first place.

But I still don't think I did anything wrong! If the sword hadn't broken, I'd be dead. If anything, Zenobia got what she deserved. Serves her right.

I hope she spends a ton of money on another fake sword. That way, it'll break if she attacks me again.

I give a nefarious chuckle, and Lady Mary turns to me to continue the conversation.

"Looks like we'll have to go to the lake ourselves. Can we?"

"I'm afraid not. Everyone who could possibly escort us has the day off. And the master ordered that you be accompanied by a guard should you go anywhere."

Lady Mary has been taking regular trips to the lake for her afternoon playtime, while also bringing sandwiches for picnics. They're a mixture of carrot and pumpkin between colorful slices of various types of bread, along with herb-roasted chicken and smoked salmon. I would love to have that again.

Oh, right. We can't have that now. That's a shame.

"Which means you will have to spend your afternoon at the mansion today."

"…Okay."

The young lady nods obediently and heads back to her room.

I huff and follow after.

"Woof, woof! *(Lady Mary! Aren't you tired from your studies? I really recommend a good nap! Naps are the best! Let's treat ourselves to doing absolutely nothing together! You can bury yourself in my fluff!)*"

I wag my tail and hop around excitedly like a good, faithful dog.

"Routa, please be quiet."

"Arf? *(What?)*"

My lady flat out refuses my suggestions and opens the window. She sticks her head out and looks around. The mansion is big, but there aren't many people who work here. I can't sense anyone, and the gardener doesn't seem to be here, either.

"No one's around. Now's our chance…"

"Arww? *(What are you doing, my lady?)*"

I stare blankly at her as she puts on a wide-brimmed hat with a flower and casually steps up onto the windowsill.

"A-arwf?! *(M-my lady?! Isn't that a little improper?!)*"

"Shh! Quiet. We're only going out for a little bit, just the two of us. It'll be fine. If we don't stay too long and make it back before lunch, we'll be okay."

Hmm. It's at least an hour's walk one way. That would take up way too much time. Plus, it's hot. We should just laze around the house.

"Come on. Let's go, Routa."

Her mind is made up. She won't listen to anyone when she gets like this.

That tomboy side of hers is peeking out again.

If I howled right now, the maid would come and put a stop to her plans, but then Lady Mary would be upset, and I don't want her to hate me. She studies hard every day; the stress must really build up. A picnic by the lake sounds fun, too.

I guess I don't have a choice. I'll go with her.

In all honesty, my lady is so headstrong that it was bound to end up this way.

"Woof, woof! *(W-we'll go for a bit, then come right back! Missing a meal is unforgivable!)*"

"Hee-hee-hee, okay. That's why I love you, Routa."

"Arwf... *(Great. So now you understand me...)*"

She holds down her skirt and hat and jumps out the window.

We're only on the first floor, so she's in no danger.

I follow her out the window.

"All right, let's go, Routa. Quietly, now."

"Woof! *(Okay, my lady. I'm great at sneaking.)*"

When I sneak into the kitchen at night to steal snacks, that is.

† † †

A (self-proclaimed) dog and girl walk along the town road between the trees.

"Phew. This is taking forever."

Lady Mary lets out a sigh.

Neither of us normally go on long walks. I may be lazy, but I'm still a dog—well, wolf—so I'm not tired at all.

"Let's rest in the shade of that tree."

"Woof! *(Sounds good! I love resting! Actually, why don't we just give up here and head back?)*"

"We're not going back."

"Arww...? *(Really...?)*"

I lie down, and mistress uses my back as a headrest, sighing. The maid normally brings her tea, but her only company at the moment is a big, useless dog. The least I can do is be her pillow. Rest well, my lady.

It's really hot out today, so the occasional cool breeze feels nice.

We rest in the shade of the tree for a while when mistress unexpectedly leans into me. I can hear her calm, even breaths.

"Arrf? (Uh-oh... Did you fall asleep?)"

She must be burned-out. She studies every day from morning to night.

"Arwf... (Hmm, nothing else to do. Guess I'll sleep, too...)"

Oh, no, I can't do that.

We need to get back before lunch, or they'll find out we left.

I can't bear to hear my lady get scolded.

I go to wake her up by poking her cheek with my nose when I notice a strange scent. It's not Lady Mary, of course. She only ever smells like flowers.

"Grwwl... (This smell...)"

I subconsciously wrinkle my nose.

This is the same scent from the carriage.

It's the smell of beasts, like dirt, filth, and blood mixed together in a putrid stench.

Where is it coming from?

"Grr...? (That way...?)"

It's coming from inside the forest. And it's getting stronger.

My large ears perk up, searching for sounds.

If I concentrate, I can clearly distinguish the subtle sounds of the birds chirping and the breeze blowing through the leaves.

My hearing homes in on the owner of the strange aroma.

"Grr...! (Found you...!)"

I can hear a group walking. My expert hearing can even tell me what they look like and how many there are.

They're pretty small. Their footsteps make them sound like they're roughly the size of children, but there are a lot of them.

Five, no six.

If I focus, I can hear them talking.

"Gyuk, gyuk, gyuk, food."

"Gyak, gyak, attack."

"Girl, girl, gehee."

…This is bad. That's them, all right. With those strange, croaking voices, there's no way they're human.

These are those monster things. Do they already know we're here? There's no hesitation in their footsteps. They're heading right for us.

Luckily, they're still a fair distance away. We need to get out of here right now.

But how?

I'll be fine, but I don't think Lady Mary will be able to escape.

What if I carried her on my back?

No, that wouldn't work. Lady Mary is in dreamland right now. She'll probably be pretty groggy when she wakes up.

Also, I'm not a horse. Even if I let her ride me, she'd probably shift around a lot on my back. There's no way I could carry a sleepy human without dropping them.

What do I do? What do I do…?!

"Grr… *(Looks like I've got no other option…!)*"

I slip out from under Lady Mary, careful not to wake her.

She looks reluctant to part ways and reaches out her hand, searching for my warmth, but she soon falls back into a deep sleep.

All right, extraction successful. Now I just need to run for it.

"Grr. *(I'm sorry, my lady.)*"

Logically, if I leave her like this, then the monsters will only go after her. Then while they're attacking her, I can make a clean getaway.

Yeah, right! You thought I'd abandon her?!

I'm heading straight for the enemy!

† † †

I run hard as I feel the tears welling up.

"Awooo! *(If anything were to happen to Lady Mary, my luxurious pet life would be oveeeer!!)*"

Damn it! That's the same as dying!

My cushy pet life has only just begun. I can't let it end here! I won't let it end!

I'm going to eat and sleep every day while my lady pets me!

Anyone who gets in the way of that is my enemy!

I'll start by chasing them out of the forest.

My target is a group of monsters.

I may have this wolf body, but I'm still me on the inside. I don't think about fighting and winning. Just chasing them out should be fine.

It'll be a bluff. I'll just pretend.

It's only been a month since I was born, but luckily, I have a ferocious face. I can use this.

First, I'll jump out in front of them; then, I'll howl as loud as I can. Then, I'll glare at them and scare the crap out of them.

I'll say, *"I could kill you all with a single bite, but I'll let you go for today. Now get out of here and never show yourselves again, you pitiful imps."* Or something grand like that.

I've got this.

I can do it.

Believe! I saw myself in that mirror. My face is scary enough to make someone wet themselves.

"Grr! *(Okay, let's do thiiiis!)*"

I pump myself up and jump, flying over the tall, overgrown forest.

The group of monsters is ahead of me. I can tell by their stench.

First, I'll howl to scare them.

I let out a huge one.

"GAROOOOOOOOOOOOOOOO?! *(Which one of you is trying to get in the way of my carefree liiiiiiiiiiiiiiiiiiiife?!)*"

My roar shakes the entire forest; leaves fall, birds scatter, and small animals faint.

At the same time, my mouth emits a beam of light, swallowing up the group of monsters among the trees.

The light is so dazzling, I have to close my eyes. Then, I open them again...

Stretching out in front of me is a circle where the forest has been hollowed out.

"...Arf? *(...Huh?)*"

I stand there, dumbfounded, and then shout in surprise:

"A-arwf?! *(D-d-did that just come out of my mouth?!)*"

Th-th-th-that was me!

Me! A wolf can't do *that*!

What the heck was that beam?! Does a beam come out if I howl as hard as I can?!

That giant pillar of light that shot out of my mouth vaporized a huge section of the forest in front of me. The ground where the trees were carved out is smooth like a mirror. It's not even burnt, more like everything in that space was just removed.

The monsters that got swallowed up in it were completely disintegrated.

So I can kill things with a single shot. I defeated them without even seeing their faces.

This body is terrifyingly strong.

"Woof, woof?! *(So? How in the world is that supposed to help me with my carefree pet life?!)*"

I didn't wish for combat abilities! I wished for a life of loafing, eating, and sleeping!!

Even a normal wolf would've been way better than this! I'm definitely a monster!

A regular beast doesn't fire lasers from its mouth!

What kind of second life did you expect me to have, you dumb goddess?!

I told you to make me a dog! Not a wolf or a monster!

A creature who's the prey, not the predator! Not a source of XP for a group of adventurers! Not a creature that can be farmed as a resource for armor and weapons! Not someone who's Monster Huuuunted!!

"Woof, woof! *(Do-over! I need a do-over!)*"

I bark at the sky, but of course, there's no reply.

"*Wheeze, wheeze... (I—I think that's enough for today...)*"

Ah. I completely forgot I left Lady Mary all alone.

If I hurry, I might be able to make it back before she wakes up. I'd better get going.

I decide to shelve the topics of my body and the appearance of monsters for now.

I go back the way I came, dashing through the trees like a gust of wind, and make it back to my lady in the blink of an eye.

"Hmm... Hmm..."

"Arwf. *(She's still asleep... What a courageous girl my master is.)*"

"Hee-hee-hee... Eat lots and grow nice and big... Routa..."

I'm pretty sure that beam I fired made a loud noise, but my lady is still in dreamland.

It'll be a problem if I get any bigger than I am now. If I could wish for anything, it would be to stop growing. But that's impossible. The old man's food is just too good! It's so frustrating! But I keep eating! *Twitch, twitch.*

I poke her with my nose while I think about what's on today's lunch menu.

"Arw. *(Lady Mary, wake up. I don't want any more of those monsters turning up. Let's get going.)*"

"U-uwha...?"

I poke her smooth cheek a few times, and she sits up, rubbing her eyes sleepily.

"Ung... Zzz..."

"Arww, arww. *(Ah, don't fall asleep now. Come on—time to wake up.)*"

Her body leans over as she buries her face in my fur, making it difficult to move.

My lady is so bad at waking up.

"Hmm…? Routaaa…?"

"Bark. *(Yes, yes, it's your lovable pet, the adorable Routa.)*"

"The lake…?"

"Woof, woof! *(Not today. Look at the sun; it's almost midday. We need to get back soon, or the maid will find out we left and won't leave us alone ever again!)*"

"Aw… That's too bad…"

I support my sleepy and slightly dejected mistress, and we head for the road back to the mansion.

We enter through the back gate and skillfully return to her room through the window.

Just a moment later, the maid calls for us. That was close.

It doesn't look like anyone noticed we were gone.

It also doesn't seem like the explosive sounds in the forest reached the mansion, either. In fact, everything has gone strangely quiet.

"Bark. *(All right, mission complete. Now it's food time! Food!)*"

I quickly head for the kitchen.

Of course, I don't run inside the mansion. I'm very smart after all! A very smart dog! Certainly not a monster! There's no way I'd be a monster!!

I weep internally as I shy away from reality.

As I get closer to the kitchen, an amazing smell slowly drifts toward me.

I let it lead me straight to the kitchen, then poke my head in.

"Arww! *(Hey, old man, I'm hungry!)*"

"Oh, there he is, the glutton. I swear I spend more time preparing your meals than the master's."

He shrugs in defeat and prepares a huge plate of food for me.

"Dearest guest, today's menu is rainbow trout *poêle à frire.*"

He jokingly bows, and I bark energetically in response, leaping for the dish.

"Gromff, omff!! *(Whoa, this is so amazing! Absolutely amazing!!)*"

When I bite into the crispy skin, fat dripping with umami spills out.

What an amazing amount of fat. It tastes almost sweet but isn't overwhelming at all.

I'm greeted by a hint of saltiness from the sauce on the plate. Even though it's extremely rich and creamy, it's been whipped full of air into a mousse, making the fragrance explode in my mouth.

"Woof, woof?! *(Hey, old man, what in the world is this sauce...?!)*"

"Hmm, what's that? You like it? I took the fond left over from sautéing some freshwater crab and mixed it with egg yolk, whisking until it foamed and stood in peaks. What do you think? Is it good?"

"Bark, bark! *(It's the best! It's fantastic! Pet me!)*"

A large hand ruffles the top of my head.

"I'm going to cook the rest of the crab up into an omelet. So look forward to that, too, okay?"

"W-woof... *(O-old man, will you not be satisfied until I'm head over heels for you...?! Oh no, I'm already madly in love with your cooking...)*"

As I lose myself in the meal, the day's events in the forest fade into obscurity.

† † †

"Arf. *(No wait, I can't forget. My cushy pet life is still at risk.)*"

After I've completely licked the plate clean, I lie down in the hall to come up with a plan.

But wow, was that lunch so incredibly delicious...

And I get to have an omelet as a snack...

"Arww. *(No, no, no, no.)*"

I can't. I have to concentrate.

I have to learn more about my body and find out why monsters are appearing in the supposedly sacred forest.

I need to head out and investigate, but that's impossible right now. Lady Mary has been taking frequent tea breaks between her afternoon studies, so if I suddenly vanish from the mansion, she'll notice and start to worry. I'll just go and patrol the forest in the dead of night.

But first things first.

I'll just take a nice long nap and rest up for later tonight.

Now then, it's the dead of night, and everyone is sound asleep.

I slip out of the bed. Lady Mary is sleeping in the big bed next to me, so I slowly wiggle away.

"Ungh... Routa...?"

She moves her hand around looking for me, probably because my warmth had vanished.

Don't worry. Sleep soundly, my lady. Don't wake up just yet.

"Routa... Routa... Hmm......"

Just as I thought, her breathing soon slows, and she's back to sleep.

"...Arwf. *(I'm just going to have a quick look in the forest. I'll be right back. Then you can use me as a pillow as much as you like.)*"

I use my front paw to open the window and leap outside.

"Arw... *(I've gotten pretty used to barking like a dog. It won't be long before I'm a real dog...! Not really. That's just a hope.)*"

If I keep insisting I'm a dog, then maybe I'll really become one someday.

"Arr... *(It's fundamentally impossible, though... Anyway, before I head out...)*"

I stand up on my hind legs and check the kitchen through the window of the back door.

Ah, old man James is slumped over, sleeping at his desk. Numerous recipes he's written are scattered around him.

"Arww. *(He's such a hard worker.)*"

He already makes such delicious meals but also stays up late into the night doing research. He's a model chef.

The old man is kind of like Zenobia. He hasn't actually been hired to work here. He's more like a welcomed guest living in the mansion on the condition that he's free to purchase ingredients as he likes.

They both seem to be personal friends of Papa.

I don't really know the details, but I do know that the old man's an amazing chef.

"Ack…Routa…you…bottomless pit…"

Whatever is going on in his dream, it seems I've made an appearance.

I'm eating even in his dreams.

He has a horrible impression of me. It's like I'm someone who doesn't do anything but eat and sleep.

Actually, I wonder what dream-me is eating… I'm intrigued. *Shlurp.*

"Hey, hey…don't eat the plate…heh-heh-heh."

I wouldn't! I wouldn't do something that ridiculous!! How can he think so poorly of me?

He must be exhausted, sleeping so soundly in such an uncomfortable position on the desk.

"Arww… *(He's going to catch a cold if I leave him like that…)*"

I enter the kitchen through the back door and reappear in the corridor a moment later. I sneak into the linen closet where the spare sheets are kept and borrow a blanket. I carry it back in my mouth and throw it over the old man. Some recipes scatter on the floor, and I pick them up and put them back on the desk.

"Arw, arw… *(Don't catch a cold now, old man.)*"

I double-check he's still asleep and go back to scrounge in the kitchen.

"Arf… *(What's that? Oh, no need to thank me. I'll just grab a little something for myself!)*"

A string of sausages is hanging on a shelf. They're my target.

Taking them was my original reason for coming, after all.

Midnight snacking sure is exciting.

I wrap the sausages around my neck into a meat necklace.

A snack is essential when you're going out. And I'm sure the old man's homemade sausages will be delicious. Boiled or fried, I don't mind, but these are smoked and perfectly edible as they are.

I never had blood sausage when I was human, but I've heard they're fantastic. You might think blood sausage would have a strong iron smell, but they don't. They're soft like pâté and have a rich flavor like eating a soup full of herbs.

And because the old man made them, they have something similar to walnuts mixed in, so there's a crunch when you bite through the skin. The meat juices and the chunks of filling come together and taste heavenly...

Ah, whoops, I'm drooling again. I can't eat them now. These are a snack for later. A snack for later.

"Arf. *(Right, then. Off I go!)*"

I leave the mansion with the sausages still wrapped around my neck, then check to make sure there's no one around before I leap over the wall.

I never thought I could jump this high before, but it's easy for me to hop over this wall that's taller than a human.

Hmm, this body really is great. Top-notch.

I might be able to handle some aggressive monsters if I encounter any.

Then again, I'm the type to run away. I can't fight. Nope, not at all. I'm pretty sure I'd lose even a verbal argument.

"Arf... *(Which reminds me. I've only just noticed, but...)*"

Isn't this Zenobia's job?!

Why am I the one looking for monsters?!

Isn't that why you're here, Zenobia?!

Why did you have to go to town to get a sword?! Get out there and slay some monsters!

Are you really that stupid?! Really?! Dumb enough to eat a plate?!

"Arww. *(Then again, Zenobia being bad is also pretty cute. Makes me want to lick her.)*"

All right then, I guess it's up to me to do something while she's not around.

I will protect my carefree pet life! I can do it! Or at least my amazing body can!

Psyched up, I lift my nose high and take a deep breath. An enormous amount of information from the various smells in the air hits me all at once.

I can smell trees and small animals. I can even smell the negative ions in a flowing stream. A multitude of aromas rushes into my head like pictures.

Nice! Way to go, nose!

Show me the amazing smelling capabilities of a dog!

Even though I'm not one!

I try sniffing the air, but the dangerous scent from before is nowhere to be found. It doesn't look like any more of those monsters are nearby. I guess I'll have a safe trip.

I'll head for the place where I fired off that mouth beam. I don't have any other clues right now.

I trot through the darkness with only the light of the moon to guide my way.

"Woof, woof. *(Whoa, walking at night is pretty fun.)*"

I slept enough during the day, so I couldn't sleep at all when night came. I might take more nighttime walks like this.

"Arf. *(Whoa, my body feels so light. How fast am I going?)*"

I'm starting to like running, and I'm getting faster and faster.

"Ha-ha-ha-ha! *(Whoaaa! I'm as fast as the wind!)*"

The scenery blurs around me, and the cool night air blowing past my snout feels amazing.

Which reminds me—when was the last time I ran as fast as I could?

I must have done it before I became a dog, but it was so long ago, I don't even remember.

"Arf! *(Running is so much fun!)*"

As my mind begins racing, I arrive at my destination before I know it.

"Bark! *(I'm here!)*"

The area is exactly as I left it. The trees are still missing, and I don't sense any animals. They're probably still afraid.

I guess for now I should look around for any more of those little monsters.

Sniff, sniff, sniff. Ah. *Sniff, sniff, sniff.*

"Arww... *(Hmm. I can't really pick up the scent. There's a little here and there, but...)*"

I sniff all around the area, but there's no strong scent anywhere. It seems what I'm smelling is just traces from the ones before.

"Woof... *(I think I'll take a break...)*"

I find a patch of overgrown grass and lie down.

"Grww. *(What a beautiful night... The moon's full, but I can still see so many stars. I wonder if it's because it's so clear. It's probably because there are no houses near here.)*"

The night sky above the pitch-black forest is so beautiful.

Then again, my incredible eyes can see easily even without lanterns. I can see so far with just the light of the stars.

"... *(Hmm? Hmmm?)*"

As I stare at the moon, a strange feeling washes over me.

"... *(Huh? What is this? Why do I feel so excited...?!)*"

So, so, so, so, so, so, so, so excited!

What is this?! What's going on?!

I don't know what caused it, but I instinctively stand up.

"Woof, woof! *(Hey, hey, hey! Why do I feel sooo exciiiited?!)*"

The moment I'm on my feet, I start racing through the forest.

I'm not thinking about what direction I'm going in, just that I need to run, and suddenly, the trees clear away.

It's a cliff. I'm out of the forest and on a cliff where I can clearly see the moon.

The rock is like a sword sticking out of the ground. I rush to the edge of the cliff and stop short.

Then I take a deep breath and…
"Awoooooooooooooooo! *(Howling feels so gooooooood!!)*"
I howl at the moon.

† † †

"Awooooooooo! Awoooooooooo! *(Ooohhhhhh gnh!! Howling feels amaaaa-ziiiing!! Soooo goooooooood!!)*"
I keep howling like that for a good ten minutes, feeling completely relieved afterward.
"Arw… *(…What the hell was that…?)*"
My sense of relief quickly turns to manic depression.
Isn't howling at the moon a wolf thing?
"Arf… *(Haah, I think it's time to go back…)*"
I've lost all motivation. I guess this is what you'd call postcoital clarity.
But I've come all this way, might as well enjoy my sausages before heading back.
Which should I have first?
The herb sausages? The blood sausages with nuts? The garlic-filled sausages look good, too.
Hang on. Isn't garlic poisonous to dogs?
I guess it'll be fine. I'm just a doglike creature, after all.
I don't know who I'm giving excuses to, but I keep looking for the best place to start on my sausage necklace.
Hmm. I might have gotten carried away and brought too many. I picked up everything that was hanging up in the kitchen……
What if the old man is furious about it tomorrow?
I completely forget my original goal and turn away from the cliff.
When suddenly…
"Awoooooooooooo!"
"Awoooooo!"
"Awoooooooooooooooo!"
…a number of howls echo around me.

"Arf?! *(Wh-wh-what?!)*"

I can hear a pack of paws moving toward me from the forest with the howling.

"Arw?! *(Huh? What?! What's going on?!)*"

As I stand there, confused, the large number of paws I can hear gets closer.

There's the cliff behind me. I have nowhere to run.

"W-woof, bark?! *(The beam?! Now's the time to use the beam, right?!)*"

Is it my turn to mow them down?!

I can fire it, right?! The beam will come out, right?! I just have to howl with all my might, right?!

Damn. I wish I'd practiced this!

The bushes in the forest start to rustle, and a number of eyes reflecting the light of the moon appear in the darkness.

Eek! Why are there so many?!

"Grr... *(I—I don't have a choice. The victor strikes first. Eat or be eaten... Here I go! Take this!)*"

I take a deep breath and feel the power well up in my throat.

"Grwwl."

"G-grwl! *(Please wait!)*" begs a voice that sounds a lot like mine.

"Grw?! *(Urghn?!)*"

I somehow manage to hold back the beam that's made its way to my mouth.

I'm surprised by how I could understand the voice intermingled with the sound of growling.

Canceling the beam made my mouth feel terrible. It's like when you're about to throw up but you force it back down. Gross.

Wait, that doesn't matter right now. What was that voice?

I look around to where the overgrowth splits, and a large shadow slowly emerges.

It's a wolf, blacker than the night with sharp golden eyes staring right at me. Its physique is the same as mine but much bigger.

Whoa, it's huge! And frightening!!

My shaking legs step backward, and the black wolf takes a step closer.

The air whooshes with a single swing of its long tail.

What a crazy aura of intimidation… This wolf is terrifying…

Huh? Does that mean that I look as scary as this wolf does?

That's bad. Everyone at the mansion must have nerves of steel! I know I'm one to talk, but you can't leave something this scary near you! I don't want to admit it, but Zenobia's right!

"Arf… (Wh-who are you? What do you want with me?)"

Maybe these wolves don't have any business with me and just came because they heard me howling?

I just have to tell them it was a misunderstanding, and maybe they'll let me go…

"Arf?! (Wait?! Are you mad because I'm on your territory?!)"

I'm sorry! I didn't know you have local rules like that!

Do you want protection money?! Do you want me to bury my face in the ground and beg?! If that's the case, I'm not too proud to beg!!

"Grwwl… (Ohhh, I knew it…!)"

Just as I think it's about to give the kill command, the black wolf speaks with a tone of admiration.

"Grwl…! (That sparkling silver fur bathed in the moonlight…! There's no mistaking it……! You're our king…!)"

"Awrf…? (Huh…?)"

What did this wolf just say?

At any rate, it doesn't seem angry, but I can't really follow what's going on anymore.

What does it mean by "sparkling silver fur"? My fur is fluffy and white.

I follow the black wolf's line of sight down to my body.

"Arf?! (Wh-why is my body shining?!)"

Huh? What is this? It looks like I'm being illuminated!

The area where the sausages were wrapped around my neck is sparkling. I look so stupid right now…

"Graow! *(My king! Our king! By the ancient oath, we representatives of the Fen Wolves have come to you!)*"

"Arww?! *(Fwah?! King?! What oath?!)*"

I didn't make any promises!!

"Grwl, grwl! *(The legend of our kind has been passed down through many generations. When a thousand years have passed, under the full moon's light, our true king—Fenrir, King of the Fen Wolves—shall return!)*"

No, no, no. I don't know anything about this. You've got the wrong wolf.

I don't remember signing a contract like that or anything.

It's null and void! A meaningless deal like that is null and void!!

"Grrrwl! *(The prophecy has finally come to fruition! Great King! Now we shall raze the forest, slaughter the humans, and restore the magical age of survival of the fittest!)*"

"Arf? *(Wait, that's the first I've heard of this.)*"

My words don't seem to reach them, and the black wolf continues excitedly.

"Grw, grwl!! *(As the oath dictated, we were to protect this forest—to chase away any humans who enter here without killing them and wait for our hidden king! However, now that our king has returned, the duty that was thrust upon us is at an end! Our rebellion can begin at last!)*"

"Awoooooooo!! *(King! King! Our true king!)*"

The black wolves respond in chorus, many more appearing around me, every one of them howling fiercely.

"Grww! *(The king's army shall be made anew this very night!! Now, great King, let us be off!! We shall topple thousands of settlements and bring about the end of humanity!!)*"

"Woof! *(No thank you!)*"

"...Grwl? *(...I beg your pardon...?)*"

"Woof, woof. *(I said nope. No thank you. I refuse.)*"

"G-grwl! *(B-but why?! The humans have grown fat and increasingly reckless, burning forests and killing animals for sport. Why would you want to allow such filth to continue walking this earth?!)*"

"Grwwl! *(Silence, whelp! I shall grant you true enlightenment!)*"

Because I live with humans! I get food! And baths! And my lady!

Foolish creatures ignorant of the wonders of civilization. I'll teach you all how amazing humans really are!

"Grrrwn...... *(M-my humblest apologies, my king! I did not mean to belittle your superiority.......!)*"

At my cry, the black wolf tucks its tail between his legs and begins crawling on the ground.

Its trembling form is kind of cute.

I drop the string of sausages in front of the wolf whose front paws now cover its face.

Phew. That's a smooth exit from looking like an idiot.

"Bark. *(Eat.)*"

"Grwl... *(Ah. N-no, I couldn't possibly... One as lowly as I cannot accept the prey of our great king...!)*"

"Woof, woof. *(Just eat it.)*"

I push the sausage with my nose.

"Grwl. *(I-if you command... Please excuse me.)*"

It nervously takes a bite out of the sausage.

"G-grwl...?! *(Wh-what is...?!)*"

Its eyes instantly widen in amazement.

"Grwl...! *(What a rich scent of blood...! There is no stench to it at all, yet it is brimming with energy... What a strong fragrance...!)*"

Looks like it ate one of the blood sausages.

Tasty, right? That's one of my favorites, too.

"Grwl...! *(Wh-what kind of animal has such meat...?! I have never eaten something so delicious in all my years...!)*"

"Woof, woof. *(That is food made by the humans you guys want to destroy.)*"

"Grwl?! *(H-humans made this...?!)*"

"Woof, woof. *(If you wipe out the humans, we won't be able to eat things like this. You must not kill them. I order you to coexist with them.)*" I puff out my chest and assert myself to the wolves.

If they wipe out the humans, there won't be anyone to take care of me.

"G-g-grww! *(I—I feel like such a fool......!)*"

Good wolf. I'm just glad you understand where I'm coming from. The old man's cooking dispels the murderous intent of wolves.

"Woof, woof. *(You should all try some; it's good. Oh, make sure you share them with everyone.)*"

The sausages are divided for everyone, leaving only a little for each wolf, but it will have to do for a taste. The lower-ranking wolves, who had been lying prostrate, rush forward for the sausages.

"Grw, grwl! *(Delicious! Amazing!)*"

"Grw, grwl! *(The king is marvelous! I can't believe humans can make something like this!)*"

"Grw, grwl, grwl! *(The king already has the humans under his control! Incredible! The king is wonderful!)*"

......Huh? Is this conversation going in a direction different than I wanted?

"Awooooooooooo!! *(Oh, King! We shall follow your will wherever it leads!)*"

"Awoooooooooooooooo! *(King! King! Our magnificent king!)*"

"Woof, woof! *(Ah, w-wait! I forgot to tell you—you're wrong! I'm not your king! I'm certainly not this Fenrir, I'm just a normal dog!!)*"

"Grw, grwl. *(Ha-ha-ha! You make the most excellent jokes, my king.)*"

"Awooooooooo! *(But I'm trying to tell you I'm not your kiiiiiiing!)*"

It looks like it's going to take some time to convince these wolves. I howl mournfully at the moonlit sky.

† † †

No matter what I say, these Fen Wolves keep barking back at me as if they don't believe me. After the moon falls a little, they finally calm down.

"Grwl, grwl. *(I have been wondering something for a while now, my king. Why is it that the noblest King of Fen Wolves chooses to speak like some common cur?)"*

So he's interested in the barking voice I worked so hard on.

"Woof, woof. *(I told you already. That's because I am a dog.)"*

"Grwl? *(Hmm? No, no, surely you jest. You are not some lowly pet of the humans. You are the proud King Fenrir.)"*

"Growl! *(Silence, whelp! I shall grant you true enlightenment! [For the second time!])"*

"Y-yipe! *(Eek! F-forgive me!)"*

The wolves all cry and shrink back, tucking their tails and lowering their bodies on the ground at the same time.

They're so cute when they hide their faces with their front paws.

Wait, I'm getting distracted.

"Woof, woof. *(Anyway. I already told you: No attacking the humans. You're going to live peacefully in the forest. I shall bring you more delicious food if you do.)"*

"Grwl. *(We follow our king's orders. Your word is law.)"*

I've already given up on convincing them. No matter what I say, they just reply with something like "The king is incredible!"

If they'll listen to my orders and behave themselves, then that's good enough for me.

Seeing them shaking with their tails between their legs, they actually aren't that scary.

"Bark. *(Oh, right. I just remembered. You guys might know something.)"*

"Grwl? *(Something about what?)"*

"Woof, woof. *(Well, there haven't been any monsters in the forest before, but the other day, these small, imp-like monsters appeared. I came out tonight to find out what they were.)"*

I also wanted to figure out what I was, but thanks to these guys, I've think I've found my answer.

Fenrir? Wasn't that some wolf from a Scandinavian legend? Seems like they have a similar story in this world. I'm sure it was something like a wolf big enough to make the earth tremble. Wasn't it also the one that eventually killed Odin?

......Hmm?

Does that mean I'll grow as big as that in the end?

That's not good, is it? That's definitely bad, right?!

"Arww...... *(No, this is terrible. Really awful.)*"

I'm a dog. I'm a dog.

As long as I think I'm a dog and act like a dog, I'm sure I'll be able to convince everyone else, too...

"Grwl. *(Goblins? We kill all monsters that show their faces in this forest, although there might be one place they're leaking in from.)*"

The wolf's voice brings me back to reality.

"Bark? *(Huh? What was that? Oh, right, I did hear the divine protection of the sacred lake keeps the monsters away......)*"

"Grwl, grwl. *(I have never heard of such a tale. We Fen Wolves have maintained our pledge for a thousand years to clear out any monsters that come out of the deep woods.)*"

So the legend about the lake was a lie.

Which means there's no giant crystal that sank to the bottom? And I'd been considering swimming down there and checking it out sometime...

But that also means it wasn't thanks to the lake that Lady Mary and everyone at the mansion have been able to live peacefully.

Nice work. I'm impressed.

"Woof, woof. *(You're amazing. You've worked very hard these last thousand years...)*"

"G-grwl! *(W-we are extremely delighted and humbled by your praise!!)*"

The black wolves lower their heads and, one by one, begin barking.

"Grwl, grwl! *(The king praised us!)*"

"Grwl, grwl! *(Oh, King! Such a benevolent king!)*"

""""Grrrrrrwwwwl! *(King! King! King!)*""""

Now, now, that's enough of that.

"Woof, woof? *(So why are some suddenly appearing after you've done such a great job?)*"

"Grwl... *(Well...)*"

The black wolf falters.

"Bark? *(Did something happen? Tell me.)*"

"Grww. *(Very well, then. I believe it would be faster to show you. I can explain on the way. Would you mind accompanying us?)*"

"Woof, woof. *(All right. But I have to get back before morning, so make it quick.)*"

"Grw! *(Yes! This way, then.)*"

The black wolf lets out a single howl, and all the others head into the forest.

I line up with the black wolf, and we venture into the dark wood.

"Grw. *(My apologies for the late introduction. My name is Garo. I am the warleader of the Fen Wolves.)*"

"Bark. *(Garo. Okay, then. It's nice to meet you. You can call me Routa.)*"

"Grw! *(You would bless us with your hallowed name…?! There is no greater honor…!)*"

"Grwl! Grwl! Grwl! *(King! King! King!)*"

I am really getting tired of these wolves' songs of praise.

"Grw. *(This is the place, my king.)*"

"Bark? *(Oh, so this is where the monsters live?)*"

We examine a spot hidden by shrubbery. It looks like a small mountain with a cave entrance jutting out of the ground. There are no monsters nearby, but I can smell and sense the creatures deep inside the cave.

"Grw. *(They do not actually live here. It is more accurate to say that this is where they spawn. Monsters are different from regular animals. They are more closely related to spirits and generate naturally from locations such as this, where magic gathers.)*"

"Bark. *(Ohhh. So they're not birthed from a mother.)*"

"Grw. *(That is correct. The cave you see before you is actually a special kind of giant monster.)*"

"Woof? *(Huh? This cave?* This *cave is a monster? It just looks like an ordinary cave to me.)*"

"Grw, grwl. *(No, that hole is alive. It takes root in places where magic gathers, expands inside the open areas underground, and keeps monsters in its belly. These creatures kill anything that enters and absorb the flesh and magic of the dead, growing ever larger. It is an incredibly dangerous monster. We call this one the Labyrinth.)*"

"Woof. *(Wow. You're incredibly knowledgeable, Garo.)*"

"G-grw! *(I—I am grateful for your praise…!)*"

""""Grwl! *(Oh, King—!)*""""

"Woof. *(Quiet.)*"

""""Arww…""""

I beat them to the punch before they could start their chorus again.

Phew. Looks like I'm getting the hang of this.

"Woof, woof? *(So this Labyrinth thing is what's causing the problems? You all look incredibly strong. Can't you go inside and just kill it?)*"

"Grwl, grwl. *(No, we cannot. The Labyrinth controls all monsters that enter it. We are no exception. Any monsters that get any closer will be assimilated.)*"

Hmm, so it's like a Venus flytrap. The fact that it controls monsters like slaves makes it even more dangerous.

"Grwl, grwl. *(Therefore, we can only observe from afar and try to block up the hole in any way we can. It is already dangerous just being this close. Can you not sense it, oh, King? The sweet fragrance that hangs in the air, drawing us in…?)*"

"Bark. *(Nope. Not at all.)*"

In fact, it stinks.

That cave reeks like a park bathroom.

If it wanted to invite me in, then it should have smelled more like Lady Mary. She smells amazing when she holds me. Haah, I miss her. I want to go home. I want to lie down next to her and fall asleep.

I think that, and yet, here I am, working. I don't get it, either.

I'd like to finish up soon and head back.

"Grwl! *(Of course! The Labyrinth could never affect someone as powerful as you…!)*"

No, I think it's simply because I know someone who actually smells good. Lady Mary's heavenly fragrance beats toilet funk any day of the week.

"Woof. *(What's the best way to resolve this…? I don't think sealing the entrance will make a difference.)*"

"Grwl. *(It would quickly return to normal if we did that. To kill the Labyrinth, you must cut down its true form, the Labyrinth core, hidden in the deepest recesses of the cave.)*"

"Woof? *(Do you know where that is?)*"

"Grwl. *(Yes. Strangely enough, the core is roughly around the entrance. If you go straight down, you will reach it shortly, but as its name suggests, the Labyrinth has stretched itself out in all directions like the roots of a tree. It is an incredibly complicated thing. It will not be easy to reach.)*"

"Bark. *(Hmm. Okay, I know what to do. You guys stand back.)*"

That nugget of information just made this a lot easier.

"Grwl! *(Ah!…No, it's too dangerous…! Any closer, and you'll—…!)*"

"Woof, woof. *(I'll be fine, just wait right there. That's an order.)*"

"G-grwl… *(Yes, sir……)*"

I leave Garo and the other wolves behind and step inside the Labyrinth entrance.

"Bark. *(Hmph. This really is no big deal. Way to go, super body.)*"

From what Garo said, the Labyrinth's weak spot is directly down from here.

Piece of cake. I have my killer weapon.

"Grwl……! *(Let's do this…!)*"

I take a deep breath and howl with all my might.

"GARUROOOOOOOOOOOOO! *(Excuuuuse meee!! But caaaan I! Destrooooy! Your hoooooome! Noooooooow?!)*"

Of course it wasn't to going to respond yes.

A beam of light appears with my howl and fires straight down.

It instantly carves a hole into the bedrock of the cave and bores its way deep into the ground.

I shut my eyes against the bright light. When I open them again and look down, I see a terrifyingly deep pit.

Did that reach it? I wonder. Maybe I should fire another one?

But before I can give firing again due consideration, an agonizing echo resounds from the hole.

The earth shakes, and the cave begins crumbling.

"Arf?! *(Wh-whoa…?!)*"

The earth echoing gets louder and louder until the sound of everything breaking apart reaches me.

It seems I can hear all the way into the Labyrinth's body.

"Bark! *(This is bad! Time to run!)*"

As I retreat, behind me, the cave entrance begins collapsing. At the last second, it seems to almost melt away into sand.

All the monsters inside were probably buried alive. Forgive me. Rest in peace.

"Bark! *(All right then, that's one problem dealt with! I'm off! I'm going to bed!)*"

The wolves rush over to me.

"Grwl, grwl! *(That was…! The Labyrinth! In just one hit…! Rejoice everyone! Our king truly is the strongest in the world!)*"

""Grwl! Grwl! Grwl! *(King! King! King!)*""

"Woof, woof. *(Okay, yes, yes. I know. I understand how you all feel. That's it, now. Time to disperse. I'm done for today.)*"

I'm tired and can't handle any more of this. I dismiss the wolves.

I look up to see that the sky is already starting to brighten.

I need to get back ASAP or my lady will wake up.

"Grwl! *(Thank you ever so much for this, my king! We Fen Wolves will follow you anywhere!)*"

"Woof, woof. *(Hmm. No problem at all; don't worry about it.)*"

I think that perhaps things will go a lot smoother if I act more regal around them.

"Grwl! *(Please at least allow me to escort you some of the way.)*"
"Woof. *(Oh, all right, then.)*"
Seems like the black wolf will come even if I say no.
I just want to get back to the mansion.
I won't be long now, my lady.
Your fluffy, cuddly pup is on his way home.

"Grwl. *(By the way, my king, I wanted to ask you about the howl you used to summon us.)*"
"Arwf? *(What now?)*"
"Grwl, grwl— *(What does 'Ooohhhhhh gnh' mean? I would be most grateful if you could tell me for my studies—)*"
"Grwn! *(Silence, whelp! [For the third time!])*"

An Encounter with Magical Dogs and Cats! ...Or So I Thought, but It Was Actually a High-Calorie Lunch!

"Arww, arww...? *(Are you sure you do not wish for me to accompany you any farther...?)*"

"Bark. *(Yep, off you go now. It'll be bad if anyone sees you.)*"

The black wolf looks back with regret in its eyes as I shoo it away.

Before we part ways, I promise I'll howl if I have need of them again.

They've worked really hard to protect the forest.

You guys work, and I'll eat and sleep in the mansion. It's a win-win situation. Huh? It's not? Well, whatever.

"Arf. *(Phew. I'm beat. My body's not tired, but I feel mentally exhausted from working so hard for the first time in a while.)*"

The sky is already starting to brighten, but it's still the middle of the night.

I need to get back to bed soon.

I don't think I'm dirty, but I shake out any dust just in case. I then sneak back into Lady Mary's room to find she's still sleeping soundly.

"Arw... *(I'm home...)*"

I murmur as I slip into bed with her. The bed feels amazingly soft and warm from her body.

"Hmm... Routa...?"

"Arw, arw. *(I'm home, my lady.)*"

"Hmm, you feel cold... Did you go out...? You shouldn't. You need a good night's...sleep..."

"Arw. *(I know. Now let's get back to sleep. You can squeeze me as tight as you like.)*"

"Ghn... You're so fluffy, Routa..."

That's because I'm bathed and brushed every day! By you and the maid!

"......I can smell......sausages...... No fair...... I want some...... Routa......hmm......"

She buries her face into my fluffy chest and soon falls asleep again.

"*Yaaaawn. (I am so tired. All I'm going to do tomorrow is eat and sleep. Nothing else.)*"

I let out a big yawn, lean my head against the pillow, and quickly fall asleep.

† † †

"Eek!"

"Woof, woof! *(Ha-ha-ha! Too easy! Easy-peasy, my lady!)*"

I dash after the ball Lady Mary threw and catch it midair.

Zenobia the knight still isn't back, so we're behaving ourselves and playing in the garden.

"Woof, woof! *(Hey, hey, hey! The pitcher's not in the game!)*"

I carry the ball back to her in my mouth.

This is so much fun. My tail is wagging like crazy.

And look at me, innocently playing fetch! I look like a regular dog! Nothing else! Fenrir, King of the Fen Wolves, is nowhere to be seen!

"Amazing, Routa! You're so fast!"

"Bark! *(I know, right? You can throw it farther if you like!)*"

"All right, then! Here I go! Hyah!"

"Bark! *(Mwa-ha-ha-ha! Super acceleration!)*"

I whiz past her, making her hair fly up. She pushes down her skirt and hair and laughs.

"Ha-ha-ha! That's incredible, Routa!"

"Woof, woof! *(Catch is so much fun!)*"

I shoot forward at high speed and catch the ball high in the air. I land and bring it right back to her.

"Hee-hee. You're such a good boy."

"Woof, woof! *(Yeah, I am! Praise me more! Pet me more!)*"

Her soft hand gently strokes my head.

Hmm, a moment of bliss.

Lady Mary calling me cute just because I fetch a ball would have been impossible in the other world no matter what I paid.

"My lady! Your meal is ready. It's time to come inside now!"

I look over to where the voice is coming from to see the young maid waving her hand from the mansion.

Oh, the older maid will tell her off for not coming over to deliver the message.

"Aw, looks like that's the end of that… I wanted to play with you more."

"Arw, arw. *(I wanted to play with you more, too… But lunch is also important! Let's read in the shade of a tree once we're done! You can lean your head against my big, strong back.)*"

I run around my disheartened master to cheer her up.

"All right, then. We'll spend some time together after lunch."

"Woof! *(Yay! I'd love to!)*"

I watch her go and then dash over to the back door of the kitchen.

† † †

"Gromff, omff! *(So good! This is delicious! There's not much meat, but it's still so good!)*"

"Bwa-ha-ha, is it good?! You're not picky, are you? You'll eat anything!"

The old man is in a good mood as he ruffles my head.

Today's menu is a hearty bacon and vegetable quiche. The flaky pastry is so stuffed that the contents are practically falling out. Egg mixed with fresh cream binds it all together. The slow bake in the oven made the surface a dark brown color, turning it more golden wavy.

Golden wavy? What am I saying?

I said it, but I'm not entirely sure what it means. It's just that delicious.

"Bark! Bark! *(Hey, old man! This is super-good! The spinach is especially fantastic!)*"

"You need to wait for meat or fish to mature for them to be good, but vegetables are best fresh. I grow all my own vegetables in my field."

"A-arwf?! *(Th-that's amazing! You even tend your own fields!)*"

He's the perfect superhuman!

He's a man who will always work hard. Master Chef James.

I'm getting shivers. He has my highest respect.

"Woof, woof! *(You're the best! And I want more!)*"

"My goodness, you really are eating more and more each day…"

He turns around and cuts another slice of quiche for me.

I love it that he'll say these things while letting me eat as much as I want.

I wait for the second helping of quiche, trying to stop myself from drooling as my tail whips back and forth.

Then…

"I. Found. You."

I hear a voice that sounds like it's coming straight from the depths of hell. Something grabs me by the scruff of my neck.

"Come!"

"A-arwf?! *(Th-that voice?! Is that the useless knight Zenobia?!)*"

† † †

Zenobia and I are alone in the garden where she tried to dispose of me before.

Ugh, what a terrifying glare. It's like she's looking into a well.

"Things will go differently this time," she swears, retrieving the sword from the sheath on her hip.

"This is a famous sword that I got for ten times the price of my last one! This sword was forged by the great blacksmith Ganche Rue! Isn't it amazing?! The shop owner just happened to be in possession of it and sold it to me!"

"Arwf… (…Oh? Well, good for you.)"

"Wh-why do you look so blasé……?"

"Pfff. (You interrupted my delicious lunch. Of course I'm going to be in a bad mood.)"

But you know, Zenobia… You say you'll protect Lady Mary, yet where were you when she needed you most? Are you even less reliable than a house pet? Where's your motivation? If you don't have any, can you just leave? I'm the only good-for-nothing freeloader in this house.

"Wh-what's with that unimpressed look……?"

"Yaaawn."

I let out a big, bored yawn right in front of the flabbergasted Zenobia.

"Woof, woof. (So is that sword just a fake, too? If you're going to come at me, do it already. It's just going to snap in half again.)"

"Y-you…! How dare you mock me…!"

Tears well up in her eyes as she raises the sword above her head.

Then she vanishes.

"Arw? (Huh?! How is she so fast?!)"

It seems like she's making a beeline for me, but I can't see her at all.

"Haaaah!!"

I sense her slicing through the air, and she brings down her sword.

The tip of the blade blurs and comes straight for the top of my head.

"A-arf! (Crap! There's no stopping it this time! Not like last time!)"

Zenobia lowers the sword with incredible speed, and it strikes me right in the middle of my skull, splitting it in two.

The sword, that is.

"Ahhhh…?!"

The blade spins through the air and vanishes among the over-growth of a flower bed.

"A-arf… *(Y-you had me going for a moment there…)*"

What was that swing…?

If that sword had been real, I would have actually died, right…?

Is Zenobia actually really strong…?

"Tch, hick, ghnn…!"

I'm still shocked when I feel something drip onto my head.

I look up to see Zenobia's beautiful face crumpled up like a child's.

"A-arf?! *(Y-you're crying?! You're really crying!)*"

"M-my sword didn't work…!"

Her face scrunches up more, and she bawls, dropping the other half of the sword and covering her face with her hands.

"A-arww, arww. *(I-I'm sorry, Zenobia. But it's your fault, too… You shouldn't have bought that fake sword…)*"

"Sh-shut up! D-don't try to cheer me—*hik*—cheer me up! I know you're hiding what you really are!"

She snaps at me before running away.

"Arww… *(Well, then… She was invited to stay here, but she actually isn't much use as a freeloader… It's no surprise things ended up this way…)*"

Her pride is in pieces…

I pick up the half of the sword Zenobia threw away and toss it into the shrubbery.

No more evidence.

Right. Let's head back and finish eating.

† † †

"Woof, woof! *(Yeah! Quiche! Quiche!)*"

I, the ordinary dog of the family, run back for my quiche as quickly as possible. It might be a little strange that I can fire beams from my mouth, but either way, I return to my plate around the back of the kitchen.

Then I see it—a face buried in my dish.

"Woof?! *(Wha—?! An intruder?!)*"

"Mrow? *(Oh? Is this your meal?)*"

The intruder, whose head is in my food, notices me and looks up.

It's a cat.

A beautiful cat with fur as crimson as blood.

Oh, so the cats in this world are red?

The crimson cat turns to me and licks her lips.

Her bloodred eyes narrow, and she seems to give me a bewitching, beautiful smile.

"Mrow. *(You have such excellent cuisine. It smelled so good that I couldn't help but try it...)*"

"W-woof! *(M-my quiche!)*"

I was really looking forward to that!

Arrrg! Arrrg!

I hope there's a little left, but when I stick my face into my bowl, I see it's been licked clean.

"Mrow. *(Tee-hee, my thanks for the meal.)*"

She moves strangely sensually as she curls her tail around.

Ugh. So cute.

I want to pet her. I really want to pet her. And rub my face against her.

H-how dare she use her powerful fluffiness against me...!

Ah no, this is wrong. I won't be tricked!

"Woof, woof! *(I won't forgive you! Give it back! Right now! Give me back my lunch! My quiche! I was looking forward to that!)*"

I bark and howl at her and beat the ground with my forepaws.

"Meow, meow. *(All right, wait. My apologies for eating your food. I'm sorry. I will bring you something delicious to make up for it. Will you forgive me then?)*"

"Woof, woof. *(...Hmm. But you're a cat. You say it'll be delicious, but it'll probably just be a dead mouse or something, right?)*"

"Mrow. *(Well, that's rude. I certainly cannot make a meal as delicious as that, but I do have confidence in my ability to make sweets.)*"

"Bark? *(Sweets...?)*"

"Meow? *(Oh, are you not a fan of sweet things?)*"

"Bark! *(I love them!* Shlurp!*)*"

But how in the world can a cat make sweets? So strange.

Thinking about it, where did this cat come from in the first place? She's a strange color for a stray, and she has skills.

"Mrow? *(Oh? Now that I look at you, you're an incredibly white beast, aren't you?)*"

Her emerald eyes staring at me narrow suspiciously.

"W-woof! *(Wh-what?! There's nothing strange about that! I'm a dog! A dog, I tell you! No matter how you look at me, I'm a dog, all right?!)*"

"Mrow. *(No, I'm sure I've never seen a dog like you before... Well, it doesn't matter. I like you. Do you want to be my friend?)*"

"Arwf?! *(Friend?!)*"

She wants to be friends? That's sudden.

I didn't have any friends for the longest time in the other world.

I would have lunch in the bathroom stalls. I would spend my breaks at my desk. And then there was the cringe-inducing *"Okay class, partner up!"*

U-ugh, my heart hurts. I'm not going to remember the other world anymore.

I considered befriending Garo and the other wolves, but they act more like servants...

"Woof. *(I—I don't mind being your friend... You're a cat, though. Do you not mind being friends with a dog?)*"

"Mrow. *(Oh my, does species matter when it comes to making a new friend? Besides, I'm not a cat.)*"

Yeah, you are.

A cat with crimson fur like that is rare, but you look like a cat to me.

"Mrow. *(Please allow me to introduce myself. I am the witch of*

Feltbelk Forest, Hecate Luluarus. I believe you and I will be crossing paths much more often in the coming days.)"

The cat bows elegantly when she says her name.

Witch?

Did she say witch?

First, it's monsters, and now it's witches.

".............."

Upon further inspection, she's definitely a cat.

Oh, I got it! She's one of those things. A familiar.

A cat who calls herself a witch.

I see.

"Bark. *(I'm Routa. I'm this family's pet. And a dog.)*"

"Mrow. *(I don't know why you keep insisting that you're a dog... So it's Routa, is it? Hee-hee, even your name is interesting. It was lovely meeting you, Routa.)*"

The crimson cat Hecate leaps into the air and lands on the branch of a nearby tree.

She didn't really jump so much as float up with some unseen power. It was strange, like she didn't weigh anything.

"Meow. *(We shall meet again, Routa.)*"

Her eyes narrow as if she's laughing, and then she fades away like smoke.

"Arwf?! *(A-a ghost?!)*"

A sultry cat who's also a ghost, who calls herself a witch, and is good at making sweets?

There's way too much going on with you!

And so I made friends with a suspicious cat.

† † †

It happened one night.

I had slept too much during the day again. Lady Mary was sound asleep, and I was left staring up at the moon.

I don't feel the urge to howl, though.

It seems that only happens during the full moon.

Then I notice a light on in the opposite wing. That's rare.

"Arf...? *(Isn't that Papa's study?)*"

He's not normally awake this late.

I guess I'll go say hi. He's been so busy lately that I haven't had a chance to see him. It's been a while since he's petted me. As a man, I really shouldn't worry whether or not he's been petting me.

I slip out of my lady's grasp and leave the room, careful not to make any noise.

The maid shouldn't be on her nightly patrol at this time. This is when I normally sneak out to get food, after all. Although the old man has been on alert since the sausage incident.

I'll give him a little space.

I continue down the corridor as I think this, turn toward the other wing, and climb the stairs to the second floor. I turn right toward Papa's study, which is just ahead of me.

"Arww, arww? *(Papa? Are you here?)*"

I tap on the door with my forepaw, and he appears.

"Oh, it's you, Routa. Are you also unable to fall asleep?"

His cheeks look slightly flushed.

There's the faint smell of alcohol.

So he's having a nightcap?

"All right then, come on in."

Papa's study is piled high with books. He must be studying hard. Although I have no idea what work he does as the head of the household.

"Would you like a sip?"

He takes a gorgeous rocks glass off one of the bookshelves. He pops the cork off the bottle on the desk and tilts it up. The amber liquid inside makes a faint, delicious *bloop* sound as he pours it into the glass.

"Here, try a bit."

Oh, Papa, you should know better than to give alcohol to animals.

I'm still gonna drink it, though!

I'm not a dog after all! No, I'm just a (self-proclaimed) dog!

I lick up some of the amber liquid from the glass he sets on the floor.

"Arf... *(Mmm... So good... What is this...? It's more delicious than the high-quality whiskey from Ginza, which is ten thousand yen a glass... I feel all fuzzy...)*"

How long has this been aged to achieve such a refined flavor?

It much be incredibly expensive. It's a high-quality spirit for sure. There's no mistaking that.

I savor the amber liquid as I drink it.

"Hmm, you seem to know how to appreciate a fine liquor. Would you like a snack with that? James whipped this up for me before he went to bed."

I sniff the food left out on the small plate, and instantly, the scent of rich honey and cheese fills my appreciative nostrils.

"Arf...! *(Oh, that certainly will be good!)*"

It's baked cheese with a white rind. The outside is baked hard, but the moment it's cut open, I can see the melted cheese inside wobble as if it were going to spill out. Honey has been drizzled on top of the cheese, which has then been garnished with a sprinkle of crushed pepper.

I can tell, even before eating it, that it's going to be delicious.

"Woof! *(I'm digging in!)*"

I wrap my tongue around the cheese slice and brazenly chew.

"Mwaf! *(So sweeeeeeeet! It's slightly pungent but also so sweeeeeeeet! The subtle notes of salt in the cheese are amazing! It's soooo gooooooood!!)*"

I am in ecstasy over this culinary masterpiece.

I have another lick of the delicious amber alcohol while the taste of the cheese is still fresh on my tongue.

"Arf...? *(What the...? This is incredible... I'm in heaven... Is this paradise...?)*"

"Ha-ha, looks like I've made a fine drinking buddy. No one around here will drink with me. I'm glad you came by tonight, Routa."

He smiles, looking slightly exhausted, and raises his own glass to take a sip.

"Something happened a little while ago, but in the dead of night, I heard this booming noise coming from the forest." He suddenly murmurs.

"Arwg?! (*Pfft…?!*)"

The moment I realize what he's talking about, I spit out my drink.

"But no one else heard it. I hope I heard wrong, but I'm still a little worried."

"W-woof… (*R-really? How strange…*)"

It was probably *that*.

He's most likely talking about the sound from when I fired my beam into the Labyrinth. Not just the beam but the sound it made when the whole thing collapsed in on itself.

"Now I find myself staying up until roughly the time of night when I first heard the noise…… Routa, you wouldn't happen to know anything, would you?"

"W-woof? (*I—I dunno. Whatever could you mean……?*)"

I give him a vacant look, my face the picture of innocence.

"………"

"………"

We stare at each other for a while. Then, finally, he leans back into his chair.

"Ha! Ha! Ha! What in the world am I saying?"

He puts his hand up against his forehead and laughs.

"Of course, you wouldn't know anything. I must be very tired. And that sound hasn't happened again since then. It was just needless worry, after all. I'm going to finish this drink off and head to bed."

"W-woof, woof! (*R-right! That's a great idea! Sleep! Sleep and forget everything!*)"

I focus on my drink instead of him.

After we finish our nightcaps and the cheese, he puts out the lantern, and we leave.

There wasn't enough cheese to satisfy me, so I sneak into the kitchen and help myself to a little of this and a little of that.

Don't worry. The old man catches me the next day.

† † †

He holds my head firmly.

"Routa. Do you know why I'm angry?"

I try to turn my face away, but I can't move an inch.

It's not because he's strong. It's his willpower. Pure willpower.

"No, you should know why without my saying anything. You're a smart boy, after all."

Old man James's face is so close.

H-he's so scary! Way scarier than Zenobiaaa!

"W-woof?! *(Wh-what?! I don't know anything?!)*"

"The smell of ham on your breath is proof enough! What are you going to do about eating all the meat in the larder? It will be another three days before provisions from town get delivered!"

Ahhh!

Are our food supplies really in that much trouble?!

"I cannot allow the quality of the master and young lady's meals to falter. The staff needs enough food to eat, too. And you, of course! I won't allow anyone here to starve as long as I'm around!"

"A-arf! *(O-old man……!)*"

H-he's so amazing.

So cool.

I admire you. More like I'm head over heels for you.

"That's why…"

He grins and pats me on the head.

"…you're going to get some more meat."

"Woof? *(…Huh?)*"

"You know the saying. He who does not work, neither shall he eat."

"Woof, woof! *(But that saying doesn't apply to pets! A pet's work is to be loved! Which means I'm already working super-hard!)*"

I bark and bark and bark, but he doesn't care.

"Which reminds me. Here is your breakfast."

He puts down my special dog plate.

But it's not my usual delicious meal.

"Arwf?! *(Huh?! That's all?!)*"

Lying on the giant plate is a single shaving of meat. The piece of grilled meat is so tiny, it's not even a mouthful.

"All jokes aside, I do not have enough ingredients. Your gluttony knows no bounds. My provisions have been decreasing at a much higher rate than expected. I had just about enough meat and vegetables to work something out for the next three days, but then you went and ate those last night."

"Arw?! *(Urk?!)*"

His words stab at me like guilt-laden knives.

"I have vegetables. And wheat. But no meat."

He bumps his clenched fist against my chest.

"You need to man up and take responsibility. If you want to eat more meat, then you have to go out and hunt it yourself. I'll prepare anything you bring back. Go out there, kill some prey, and bring it back. You'll be fine. You can work something out. Bring out those natural wild instincts!"

"Bark! Bark! *(No, no, no, no! No way! It's impossible! I don't have any wild in me! My ancestors were all pets! I've never felt the call of the wild even for an instant!)*"

"Go forth and conquer, Routa! Until you bring back some meat, you'll just have to go hungry! I'm not kidding around here! I didn't even eat anything last night! I'm starving!"

"Arrrrww!! *(Whaaat?! You didn't eat anything?! Now I have to go! Nooooooooooooo!)*"

† † †

"Take care, now! Make sure you bring back a big one!"

"Afuu…… *(Seriously……)*"

The old man waves me off, but my crestfallen tail has no energy to wag.

My head hangs low as I leave the mansion feeling the old man's expectations bearing down on me.

"Arw... *(Haah, what should I do...? I've never hunted before...)*"

I continue trudging along when an idea pops in my head.

"Bark! *(I know! I have those guys for times like these!)*"

I'd forgotten I have some skilled allies. Hunting professionals.

"Awoooooooo! *(Garo! Gaaaro! Are you there?! I need you!!)*"

I let out a loud howl that would travel far.

"Grwl! *(At your service, my king!)*"

The black wolf's face suddenly appears behind me.

"Arwf?! *(Whoa?!)*"

When did—?!

"Bark! Bark! *(That was fast! That took you no time at all!)*"

"Grwl. *(I have been trailing you since you left, my king.)*"

What? Like a stalker?

Now that I've got a good look, I can see a few other wolves waiting behind Garo.

It's a gang of stalkers.

"Woof, woof! *(Also, your face is terrifying. Don't pop up out of nowhere like that. You startled me.)*"

"G-grwl...? *(I-it's terrifying...?)*"

Garo looks incredibly hurt by my offhanded comment and stares at the ground.

"Grw, grw! *(Excuse me, my king!)*"

One of the wolves behind Garo steps forward.

"Grw, grw! *(I am Bal! Lady Garo here is one of the most beautiful wolves in our clan! Surely she is deserving of much better—!)*"

"Grwl. *(Stand down, Bal. Please excuse my subordinate, my king. And please forgive me for appearing before you with such an unsightly visage...)*"

"Woof? *(Huh? Garo, you're female?!)*"

"Gaww...! *(Aw...!)*"

Garo lies down on the ground as if stabbed in the heart.

"Grrrww! *(Y-your majestyyyyy?! Please stop! Your words are far too careless!)*"

Bal's subservience falters as he barks in Garo's defense.

"Grwl! Grwl! *(Lady Garo is the most beautiful wolf in the entire world! Yet you state that you only see her as a male?!)*"

Ohhh, so that's it.

Garo is looking away, letting out a sad, whine-like cry.

I look at them and give them my honest opinion.

"Woof... *(You say that, but I can't tell the difference between any of you...)*"

"Grrrrrrrr?! *(Your Majestyyyyy?!)*"

Bal goes into a frenzy, saliva flying everywhere.

Ew, gross.

"Bark... *(B-but you see, I'm not a furry or anything like that...)*"

"Grw? *(F-fur...ry.......?)*"

A furry is someone who *really* loves beasts.

I'm not like that.

"...Grw...grw... *(It's fine. Just drop it, Bal. Please forgive me for showing you my gruesome face. I shall stay far away from you as you conduct your business. A thousand pardons...)*"

Garo staggers to her feet, her head still bowed.

"W-woof, bark. *(Oh no, I'm the one in the wrong here. I'm sorry. I didn't know you were such a beauty. I didn't mean to say anything hurtful to you... I'm sorry, Garo.)*"

"Grwl... *(N-no, no. It's fine. Please forgive me for losing my composure.)*"

She hasn't really accepted my apology. Her hackles are up as she sits down in front of me.

"Grw. *(Let us start again, my king. What is it you wish of us today?)*"

Looks like we're just going to have a normal exchange.

"Bark. *(Um, well. This is embarrassing to say, but I need your help with something...)*"

I'm acting very self-conscious about the whole thing as I say this to Garo, licking my nose all the while.

"Grwl! *(Oh, do you perhaps wish to leave the forest and invade the human world?! The order to subjugate the humans is finally here!)*"

"Bark! Bark! *(No! No! No! That's not it! We're not doing that!)*"

"Grw... *(Oh, I see...)*"

Why does she look so disappointed...?

These guys really are ferocious beasts deep down...

"Woof. *(I actually have a really shameless request.)*"

"Grw. *(Very well.)*"

"Woof, woof? *(Can you help me do a little hunting? And by help, I mean, can you hunt for me? Instead of me?)*"

I'll leave all the work to the wolves and enjoy the spoils myself!

See. This is the perfect plan I thought of all by myself.

Relying on others is my creed!

"Grw...! *(O-ohhh...! That is a splendid idea!)*"

Garo seems impressed.

"Grw! Grw! *(Rejoice everyone! His Highness will be leading us in a hunt!)*"

"Arf?! *(Huh?!)*"

No! No! Weren't you listening?!

You'll be doing the hunting. *I'll* be doing the eating.

Right?!

"Grw! Grw! Grw! *(King! King! Our strong king!)*"

The increasingly large pack of wolves breaks into a chant.

"W-woof?! *(Huh?! Wha—?! Wait!)*"

"Grwl. *(Now, now, my king, this way. We actually had a powerful monster spawn recently. It will be perfect. You must show us your wonderful skills!)*"

"Woof?! *(Garo?! Lady Garo?! Are you mad at me?! Are you actually furious with me?!)*"

"Grwl, grwl. *(Not at all. I would never do anything as inappropriate as express anger toward you, my king.)*"

"Woof, woof? *(Yeah, but...you're mad at me, right?)*"

"Grwl. *(Noooo, not at all. I merely wish to see you in action and revel in your magnificence.)*"

"Woof, woof! *(Liar! You're clearly still furious about what I said before!)*"

Crap! This lady knows how to hold a grudge!

"Grw. *(Now, my king, let us be off. We shall all bask in the majesty of your abilities.)*"

"Arrrrwwww!! *(Noooo! They're going to be way too strooooooooong!!)*"

I'm only somewhat on board with this as I get dragged away by the wolves.

† † †

"Fwgaaaarrrr!!"

The forest shakes.

Not a single plant remains where the giant body charges through.

Trees are knocked over, flowers are uprooted, and the grass is flattened.

All because of the giant living cannonball.

"Grw... *(I believe this should suffice for a meal.)*"

The wolves are all drooling.

What? That's your reaction to this monstrosity?!

I'm getting dragged along by wolves who lack any sense of modesty.

"Bwaaaarrrr!!"

Steam bursts from its ears, and the giant wall of flesh shakes its head.

A large splinter stuck in its furry hoof is finally shaken out.

It's a giant boar.

Isn't this thing just a bit *too* big?

It must weigh a ton. Four curved tusks longer than swords can be seen jutting out of its lower jaw. The furious boar's mucus-encrusted eyes are bloodshot with rage as it tries barreling through the surrounding wolves.

It's huge. It's just plain huge.

I'm pretty big myself, but when I look up, all I can see are the muscles rippling off this thing's back as it towers over me.

It must be the size of a house. And if that wasn't bad enough, this colossal porker can also move incredibly fast. The wolves would get blown to smithereens if they were hit by its charge.

"Grwl. *(It's fine as long as you don't get hit.)*"

The other wolves seem to share her composure. They surround the boar, making sure to keep their distance, and provoke it with howls. The giant boar then charges with blind rage, but the wolves quickly leap out of the way. The only things getting blown to smithereens are the trees.

At least this natural disaster is kicking up a nice breeze.

But this whole area will be destroyed if we let the boar rampage much longer.

"Woof, woof? *(How do you kill something like this?)*"

There don't seem to be any casualties among the wolves, but I'm also noticing a distinct lack of finishing blows to put an end to this encounter.

"Grwl, grwl. *(A monster like this is strong, so we continue to enrage it. We will run around it for three days straight until its strength gives out and it can no longer move. Then, we all bite at its nose and mouth until it can no longer breathe.)*"

"Bark… *(O-ohhh. Impressive…)*"

Wow, that's super-practical.

No mercy whatsoever.

Any animal would die if you prevented it from breathing.

Upon closer inspection, I can see they've calculated how to encircle it and are regulating fixed distances away from the boar.

The boar, which can only think of violence, is being led by the nose.

"Grwl. *(At this rate, we should have it dead in a day.)*"

They're amazing. They're professionals. Professional hunters.

"Grwl… *(Well then, my king…)*"

"W-woof? *(Y-yes?)*"

"Grw! *(…He's all yours!)*"

What?!

"Grwl! *(Clear a path, everyone! His Majesty shall fell the foul beast!)*"

Garo's voice rings out, and the pack around the boar retreats. They create a pathway by falling back to either side of the beast, leaving me in its direct line of sight.

"Grwl! *(And now, you diminutive demon piglet! One untainted by evil stands before you! Rejoice! For you have the esteemed pleasure of being vanquished by our glorious leader!)*"

Whoa! Whoa! Whoa! Garo?! Seriously, Garo?!

Why are you provoking it even further?!

The boar is already fuming!

It scrapes at the ground with its front hoof, getting ready to charge!

"Grwl. *(The preparations have been made, my king. Please slay this beast however you see fit.)*"

Don't be ridiculous!

I thought she was just getting me back for what I'd said before, but her eyes are brimming with respect. She's serious about this.

She really believes from the bottom of her heart that I can kill this boar.

I don't need your faith!

Doubt me! Doubt my strength! You'll be a lot better off that way!

If I run right at this thing, I'm absolutely going to die. This isn't like Zenobia's useless swords.

This isn't right! This whole situation is messed up! I should be living a spoiled life in a mansion, eating and sleeping! Why am I out here monster hunting? I wanna go home! I wanna go home and eat and nap! But wait…there's no food!

If I throw a tantrum and express my unwillingness to fight, Garo and the others might kill it for me. But she mentioned that their strategy could take a whole day.

Nobody's got time for that.

I'm so hungry, I could just about keel over.

I just have to kill it quickly and get back. Then James can cook me some delicious food.

That means I have to fight it.

Otherwise this fear and hunger will be all for naught!

This is getting intense.

I know. This thing isn't some terrifying monster. It's just meat, pork of the highest quality.

Just imagine it. The old man's going to cook this prime game into a whole bunch of…!

I can see it now: Grilled boar full of juicy collagen cooked into the finest dish.

I can already taste the succulent strips of pink flesh!

Shlurp.

I can't stop drooling.

I want meat. I want to eat it right now.

That's good. I'm starting to feel like I can do this now.

My gluttony is overcoming my fear!

Let's do this, super-body! Let's show these wolves our killer technique!

"Fwgaaaarrrr!!"

I don't know if it could sense my ambition, but the boar kicks off into a run.

There's so much power in its movements that it whips up a cloud of dust.

I don't move an inch.

I bury my feet into the ground and lean forward.

Let's do this, boar!

I'll take you down!

"Garooon…… *(Little Beam!)*"

Let me explain.

The Little Beam is a killer technique I developed based on my regular beam that can take out an enemy in one hit while having a bit less impact, cultivated through trial and error by gathering my will-power and letting out only a tiny howl, resulting in a much narrower beam. *(Deep breath.)*

My goal is the boar's meat. I don't want to vaporize it.

Hey, you brazen boar. Can you just die and give me your meat already?

A small beam fires out of my mouth with my howl. The white streak of light surges forth and hits the boar right in the middle of the forehead. It pierces the beast's skull like a hot knife through butter before promptly shooting out of its rear end.

"Oink?!"

A second later, the boar falls to its knees, dead.

It stays in that position as it skids along the ground and slows to a stop right in front of me.

"A-arf. *(I—I did it.)*"

"Grrrrrwl! *(What a magnificent technique! Our king truly is amazing!)*"

Garo lets out a joyful cry from her spectators' spot.

""""Grwl! Grwl! Grwl! *(King! King! King!)*""""

The other wolves begin chanting as usual.

But it doesn't bother me this time.

"Woof, woof! *(Oh, right! I need to hurry! I don't have much time!)*"

"Grwl? *(What do you mean you don't have time?)*"

Garo tilts her head to the side. Sadly, it's very not cute.

"Woof, woof! *(It's something the old man told me before I left to go hunting!)*"

"Now listen up, Routa. If you do manage to take down an animal, you need to bring it back here right away. If you don't drain the blood from your kill, it can cause the meat to smell. You do want some delicious meat, don't you?"

Yes, I do!

But how am I going to carry this huge beast back?

Could I drag it…?

"Grw. *(Is this 'old man' the human who watches over you? … We can carry this to him for you.)*"

I nod enthusiastically at her invitation.

"Grwl! *(All right everyone, this is the king's order! Pick this up! Quickly, now!)*"

""""Grw! *(Yes, ma'am!)*""""

The wolves move as one at Garo's command, crawling under the boar and lifting it up all at the same time.

"Woof! *(Whoa, amazing!)*"

The combined strength of a dozen wolves is easily sufficient to lift the giant boar.

"Grwl! *(Let's go! As fast as you can! Let's not keep His Majesty!)*"

""""Groooooowl!""""

With the carcass on their backs, the wolves howl, then run like the wind into the forest.

† † †

"Wh-wha-what the hell is thiiiiiiiiiiiiis?!"

Old man James screams in astonishment as he looks up at the mountainous boar.

We left it waiting for him outside the back door of the kitchen, so it's no surprise he screamed.

I'm pretty sure he just wet himself a little.

"R-Routa. Did you really hunt this? This huge beast…?!"

"Woof, woof! *(Yep! Aren't I amazing?!)*"

I bark proudly next to the boar.

Well, Garo and the other wolves wore it down for me.

But I'm the one who killed it with my beam.

"I'm amazed you killed such a behemoth… I would have been over the moon if you'd brought back a rabbit…"

He ruffles my head, still looking up at the beast.

"Grwl! *(You! How dare you lay your hand on the king! Such insolence!!!)*"

"Arwf?! *(A-ah, wait, didn't I tell you not to come out yet?!)*"

Garo leaps out from the shadow of the boar before I can warn her off.

"Whoa, what the—?!"

The old man steps back in surprise.

"Woof! *(Tch. Change of plans. You guys, get out here!)*"

The pack of wolves appears on my command.

There are only about fifteen of them, but seeing as they're all larger than I am, it's a pretty amazing sight.

"Ahh?! Wh-who are you guys?! Don't tell me you're wol—"

Now! Just like we practiced on the way back!

One, two, three!

""""Grr-woof, woof!"""""

"......Oh, you're all dogs..."

The old man wipes the sweat off his brow.

We did it!

I strike a victory pose in my mind.

The old man seems as blissfully ignorant as ever. He's so surprised that he's completely taken in.

"Are these your friends, Routa?"

"Woof, woof! *(Yep! They helped me hunt it!)*"

"I see. You all worked together to bring this down."

He walks up to the line of wolves.

"Grwwl! *(L-lady Garo! Stand down, old man! Don't you dare lay a hand on the princess, filthy human!)*"

The brown wolf Bal jumps forward just as James is about to pet Garo.

"Woof, woof! *(Hey! Bal! Heel! Get ahold of yourself!)*"

"G-grw...... *(Y-your Majesty... V-very well.)*"

Bal's ears flatten when I tell him to stop.

"Oh, what's this? Do you want some pats, too?"

He crouches down in front of Bal and ruffles his head with a big hand.

Bal wrinkles his nose menacingly but can't move because of my command.

"G-grwl... *(As a proud soldier of the Fen Wolves...! This insult is...! I-I'll kill you!)*"

"There. Good boy. You worked so hard! I'm impressed!"

"G-grr! *(S-stop...! Were it not for the king's order—! You would* be…! I—I can't believe I must yield to a human…! Th-this is, this iiiiiiiiiiis…!)"

The old man started at the head and is now rubbing both his hands around Bal's cheeks, until Bal finally sounds like he's going to melt, then collapses on the ground.

That must have been his first time being petted.

I think he just closed his eyes because of how good it felt…

"But you know, now that I've had a closer look at this boar, it's not a monster, is it…?"

The old man stands up and touches the boar's coarse bristles, expressing his doubt.

"And all these dogs managed to take it down… Where did you all come from? Do you live in the forest?" he asks.

Damn it. We managed to trick him so far, but he's beginning to doubt us again.

We'll be in trouble if he reports us to Papa or Zenobia…!

"Oh my, no need to worry about them," says a bewitching female voice.

When did she get here? A woman with a wide-brimmed tri-cornered hat is suddenly standing next to the old man. She tucks her long silver hair behind her ear and smiles at him. She's a real voluptuous witch.

"O-oh…! Miss Hecate. Oh my, is it that time already?"

It seems the old man is acquainted with this strange, sexy lady who appeared out of nowhere.

He quietly nods as if he knows something.

Hmm? Hecate? …Where have I heard that name before?

"These creatures are my friends. Be at ease."

"I see, so they're like your familiars? That's good, then."

"Grwl! Grwl! (Who's your friend?! We're not familiars, you infernal witch!)"

Garo growls at her.

So Garo knows this lady, too? Looks like they don't get along.

"Woof? *(Who's this?)*"

I stand next to Garo and whisper to her.

"Grw. *(She's an elf witch who lives in the western part of the forest. She just built a house and took up residence there one day... We've tried to chase her out, but...)*"

"Woof. *(So you were beaten at your own game.)*"

"Grwl! *(No! There's no way we would ever lose! But this witch uses strange illusion magic. Her sorcery always confuses us...)*"

"Woof. *(Hmm. Well, that's fine. Just let her live there. This whole land belongs to Papa either way.)*"

As his beloved dog, it's natural for me to protect what's his.

"G-grwl! *(But—! My king!)*"

"Woof, woof. *(You shouldn't be so stingy. The forest is huge. And it looks like she's a friend of the old man. There shouldn't be any issue with a few other people living in the forest. It's decided.)*"

"Grwl...... *(Very well. If that is what the king wishes...)*"

She bows her head in acquiescence.

Everything she says makes her sound so selfish.

I need to change that.

Actually, this lady doesn't seem as bad as Garo was making her out to be.

She did just save us, after all.

Getting a better look at this sexy lady reveals that she has emerald-green eyes. Just as I'm considering how nice they look, she gives me a mischievous grin.

Hmm? Hmm? I can't shake the feeling that I've seen those eyes somewhere before...

"So these guys are all familiars. Then this boar is..."

The witch smoothly dispels his doubt.

"A creature that was warped by a stray drift of magical energy, a common occurrence. These drifts can come in from anywhere, you know."

"Ohhh, so it was a monster after all... I'd heard monsters don't appear in this forest, but maybe I should alert the master just in case…"

"Do not fear. These children will dispatch any monsters that turn up. I can tell Gandolf if you'd prefer."

"Ahhh, right then. So it's thanks to you guys that the forest's safe."

The old man praises them by petting Bal on the head.

"G-grw… *(P-please stop…)*"

He's unable to move because the pats feel so good, so he tries to retreat by lying down.

"Hmm, I never imagined I would get this much monster meat. Is it even safe to eat monster meat…?"

"There aren't any adverse effects in particular. They are creatures that form when magic binds to a soul. When they are alive, that's one thing. When they are dead, though, they're no different from regular animals."

She quells his worries in an instant.

"Well, in that case, I guess I'll have to face this challenge as a chef. It may be dead, but we can still give it a delicious send-off."

He crosses his arms and closes his eyes. Then they snap open.

"Right, you guys! I require your aid! We won't be having just any old meal this time. This shall be a true testament to culinary excellence!"

Yippee!

Old man James really is the best!

I can hear the soothing sounds of the babbling brook.

Gentle rays of morning sun filter through the trees. It will still be a while before the sun is high in the sky.

"All right, then. We'll butcher it here."

The old man had pulled a cart loaded with all his tools and stopped at an open area next to the river.

I didn't know there was such a beautiful brook so close to the mansion.

The wolves carrying the boar let it down with a *boom*. The giant carcass rolls to the water's edge.

The beast is so huge that it was impossible to butcher it at the mansion. There's lots of water here, and it will prevent the mansion's residents from seeing the wolves. Although, when I think about how oblivious they are, I imagine everything would be fine if they saw them.

But it's better to be safe than sorry!

Especially with Zenobia running around. If she crossed paths with one of these wolves, there's no way it would end well.

"Hmm. It's so heavy; draining the blood is going to be an issue. It's been a while since its heart stopped, so we're going to have to find a way to get it off its side…"

The old man frowns, looking troubled as he holds a massive knife.

We could throw a rope over a branch and use that to hoist the body, but there doesn't seem to be any trees that could bear the weight.

"Oh, so you just need it hung up?"

The witch Hecate, who accompanied us, pops her head out from behind the boar with her question.

"Yes. Do you have any ideas?"

"Tee-hee, what about this?"

Hecate pulls out a metallic wand. The large jewel adorning the tip begins glowing, and the boar's giant body floats into the air as if lifted by invisible hands.

Whoa! Amazing! Magic's incredible!

Its hangs from its back end, with its head toward the ground. It stays fixed in the air as if it were hanging from a tree.

"Well?"

"My, this is something! They don't call you a witch for nothing!"

It really is incredible, but if she could have done that, then she could have helped carry the thing right from the start.

All the wolves that carried that thing are looking over, panting.

"Oh, no. Holding it in place is easy; carrying something like this would have been much more difficult. And I don't like breaking a sweat."

Hecate says this as if she just read my mind.

She stabs her wand into the riverbank to keep the boar in place, then moves over to stand beside me.

"Tee-hee."

"...Arw. *(Y-you're too close, lady.)*"

She flashes me a cheeky grin and a sideways glance.

She has a fine nose, long ears, silver hair, and an erotic aura about her. I'm sure I wouldn't forget such a unique person if I'd met her before. This is definitely the first time we've crossed paths, but I still feel like I've met her somewhere before. The way she smiles, as if she can see right through me, makes her appear as mischievous as a cat.

Huh? A cat?

Wait? Could she be...?

"I did tell you I wasn't a cat, didn't I, Routa?"

She flashes me a knowing smile.

"I see you finally noticed. I was a little sad that you didn't put it together sooner. We are friends, after all."

"Woof, woof?! *(No, but... Whaaaat? You're really the cat from before?!)*"

I'd thought she was a cat who was just calling herself a witch, but she's the real deal! If this is her real body, then did she transform into the cat from before?

"I didn't quite transform. I'll tell you about my little trick later."

With that, Hecate's gaze moves back to the old man challenging the boar with his massive knife.

The way he handles the blade is truly spectacular. It's a different kind of mastery from cutting down enemies with a sword, and before long, the giant boar has been turned into familiar chunks of meat.

The look in the wolves' eyes as they watch is otherworldly. Drool flows from their mouths, and their tails are kicking up clouds of dust. Even the proud wolves are no match for the old man. All they can do now is be patient. Hold it in until we're served an amazing meal.

"Hee-hee, what spectacular skills."

Hecate looks like she's in a trance as she praises the old man. Hearing him receive praise makes me happy, too, for some reason.

"This much meat should last the mansion quite a while..."

He says this admiringly as he looks up at the pile of pork.

It must weigh close to a ton. What an incredible amount of food.

The mountain of meat literally looks like a shrine.

"Of course, all of you helped catch it; you'll get your fair share, too. But even you couldn't eat all this in one go. I'll smoke half of it. That should help get us through winter."

That's a good idea.

His smoked meat tastes amazing. The smoked suet he once made was incredible. It had a solid texture, which melted sweetly in your mouth, slowly spreading the umami over your tongue until it completely dissolved.

It was pure magic.

I wonder how the boar meat will taste once it's been smoked.

I'm getting excited now.

Ah, but that's for the future. My hunger right now is more important.

Old man! Hurry up! Hurry up and give me some food!

"To be honest, curing this will make it a lot more delicious. It will need at least three days in a cool, dry room. But you can't wait that long, can you?"

"""Grwl! Grwl! Grwl! Grwl!!"""

The wolves voice their agreement.

Excuse me, everyone, your disguises are slipping. That should be "Woof, woof."

"I'll simply grill some of it. That'll be best."

He goes to the river and picks up some rocks, makes a hearth, then places a large, flat metal plate over it.

"The meat's still tough, though, so I'll cut it thin and grill up a big batch. I'll cook a bunch of loin, rib, and thigh. You can eat to your hearts' content."

"…Gulp… *(Y-you mean…)*"

H-he's making barbecuuuuuuuuuuue!!!

Yahoo! Routa loves barbecue!

The old man takes out a thin knife and begins carving up the meat, laying each slice onto the hot plate with the edge of the blade. As the pink meat sizzles, he flips it over, and the strips slowly curl as the fat drips away.

The wolves, who have never had barbecue before, watch the spectacle unfold in front of them, eyes glistening.

The meat dances on the hot plate, giving off an incredible smell.

It's amazing. Everyone is drooling.

Me, too, of course. I want to stick my face into the fragrant smoke.

The thin strips are soon cooked through, and the old man quickly removes them from the hot plate. Now all that's left is to serve it up.

The crisp victuals are slowly loaded onto a giant plate until a tower of meat stands before us.

""""Grwl! Grwl! Grwl! Grwl!!""""

"Whoa, hold your horses. I have to do the finishing touches."

He holds the howling wolves back, then produces a knife different from the one he just used to slice up the meat. With his other hand, he takes out a large wheel of cheese. He puts the cheese, solid enough to be used as a blunt weapon, under the hot plate and grills it over the fire. The hard cheese begins melting over the flames.

The cheese is now so soft that it bubbles. The old man prunes off slice after slice and lays them atop of the tower of meat. The barbecued boar is now blanketed by a layer of gold.

Amazing! It's calories covered in more calories!

It's not every day the old man cooks something so fattening it could kill you!

It looks so incredibly unhealthy!

But that's just fine with me!

The rich fragrance of the gamy meat and the bouquet of warm cheese combine to create an aroma so delicious that I might even consider going out hunting again!

The eyes of the wolves creeping closer and closer are getting scary. Their noses are sniffing, tongues are lolling out, and their breathing is ragged.

They never had such a look in their eyes when they were hunting the boar.

If they have to wait any longer, some might start dying of agony.

"All right, then—dig in!"

The moment he gives the okay, the wolves dive into the plate, tails wagging.

I figured it wouldn't be hot anymore, but the meat has been sliced so thin that it's the perfect temperature.

""Grwl! Grwl! Grwl! *(Delicious! Amazing! Humans are incredible!)*"""

The wolves are completely engrossed in the grilled meat and cheeses.

"Grwl! *(Y-you guys! The king has yet to dine! How dare you lay your paws on that! Et tu, Bal?!)*"

Garo barks angrily at the pack, but no one is listening.

I get it. Social rankings don't matter when the old man's cooking is involved. I forgive you. Eat to your hearts' content.

"Woof, woof! *(Which reminds me. Old man! Bring some meat over here! Garo, come sit by me!)*"

"What's that? You want to share with this black wolf? You flirt."

No, that's not it.

I'm not a furry.

"G-grw! *(H-human…! What vulgar— Th-the king and I would never—)*"

She says that, but her tail is half wagging.

"Bark. *(No, Garo, it's fine. Let's get some food.)*"

I've been holding back, but I'm at my limit now, too.

Garo and I eat the cheesy meat from the same plate.

"Mwaf?! *(Th-this is…?!)*"

Delicious!! Absolutely delicious!!

The wild boar's meat is bursting with a flavor that is perfectly accompanied by the sweetness of the cheese, overflowing with umami.

To think something so simple could be so delicious.

"Grwl…! *(Th-this is…! The same sensation as when we had the mysterious meat you brought us…! No—it may be even more wonderful…!)*"

It's so delicious even Garo is engrossed. She's completely forgotten her embarrassment and is inhaling the meat.

Which reminds me, Hecate's being quiet.

As I look around to see what she's doing—

"It is quite delicious," she says, enjoying her own plate of food.

I think she started eating before us.

She's even piling on more cheese with some pepper.

A little bit of cheese drips from her mouth as she chews with an expression of pure bliss. It really reminds me of that crimson cat.

So this witch is a big eater, too. You wouldn't think so at first glance, but she's actually pretty childish.

This is how our early lunch went. We kept eating until our stomachs were about to explode.

† † †

"Wh-what the hell is thiiiiiiiiiiiiis?!"

Later, we had to make multiple trips to the mansion to carry back all the meat, but that's another story.

I'm nervous.

I'm nervous, waiting outside my lady's bedroom.

"Dr. Hecate."

"Yes, Miss Mary?"

"That tickles."

"Oh my, this tickles? Then what about here?"

"Ha-ha-ha, stop! You're such a mean doctor!"

I can hear Lady Mary and the witch Hecate's conversation on the other side of the door.

Wh-what is going on in there?

My imagination is running wild.

By the way, Papa is right next to me, no doubt sharing the same worries.

No, he's probably worried for other reasons.

"You may enter now. I've finished my examination."

At that, Papa immediately opens the door and enters the room. He spins around so fast, the floor squeaks.

I peek into the room after him.

The maid is fussing around, tidying away my lady's clothes that litter the floor.

"H-how is she, Dr. Hecate?! My daughter... What's wrong with my daughter?"

"Please calm down, Gandolf."

Papa is practically clinging to Hecate as he grills her with questions.

Seeing a man as impressive as Papa reduced to a nervous wreck is really amusing...

"Arwf?! *(...Huh? Wait, she's sick? My lady is ill?!)*"

Hecate is molding her hair into funny shapes as she responds.

"She gets this illness every year. She'll probably get a fever within the week that will last about a month."

"I—I see......"

Papa slumps his shoulders, looking dejected.

What? My lady is going to be in bed for a whole month?! Isn't that really bad?!

"Give her this medicine three times a day. Measure the doses out precisely and make sure she takes it only after eating."

From her bag, Hecate produces a bottle filled with a glowing blue liquid and hands it to the maid.

"I'll come by every day to check up on her, so all that's left is to let her rest so she can heal."

"I understand. I'll follow your instructions to the letter."

The maid carefully takes the medicine from Hecate.

I can tell by their behavior that the mansion staff really respects her. Even the distinguished Papa acts humble around her.

Even though she's a gluttonous witch.

Everyone calls her "Doctor," so I suppose she at least has medical skills.

"Dr. Hecate. I know I shouldn't be saying this, but I am actually looking forward to seeing you every day."

"Oh my. I am honored."

My lady is the complete opposite of Papa and actually seems excited.

"And please allow me to introduce the newest member of the family to you. This is Routa."

Ah, she finally noticed me.

I quietly creep up next to Lady Mary and sit down beside her.

"Oh, we've met. Routa and I are already good friends."

"Really? You already knew about him? I was hoping to surprise you, but you two became friends even before I had the chance to introduce you. Routa, you traitor."

"Arwf?! *(Huh?! That's not it! This is a misunderstanding, my lady! You will always be my number one!)*"

"Hmph."

She looks away, puffing up her cheeks.

"Arww, arww! *(Oh no! Please believe me! Look! Routa loves his master!)*"

I edge up to Lady Mary in a panic, and Hecate giggles cheekily.

"That's right. Routa loves Mary."

"Heh-heh. I love you, too. I'm just teasing you. Sorry."

She hugs me tightly.

This is bliss. She's so soft, and she smells so nice.

I'm consumed by a sense of euphoria.

Geez, why did I panic in the first place?

Maybe because Lady Mary is really good at teasing me.

I made a vow that I would be her pet for the rest of my life. At the same time, I also vowed I would live a life as a useless degenerate.

"So we have one more week until her sickness takes full effect... I'm glad the food provisions arrived in time."

The old man lets out a sigh of relief after hearing everything from the maid.

We're in the dark, cooler room in the basement of the man-sion. It's so cold that it acts like a refrigerator, even though it's early summer. I have no idea how it works. Maybe it's kept cool with some kind of magical tool?

I prefer the fire in the old man's kitchen. It seems like magic has already bled into every facet of life here. Having never been away from the mansion, though, I honestly can't say. Not to mention Hecate is the first person I've seen use true magic spells.

"H'yup. Let's finish this up, then."

The old man hangs up the last of the meat in the cooler.

The chunks of meat, wrapped in boiled, sterilized cloths and distilled in alcohol, are going to be left in here for a while to cure.

"This meat sure is going to make some fine dishes, but it's not good for a sick person. I'll have to come up with some meals that are good for the digestion."

He's already thinking up new recipes like always.

"*Mumble, mumble...* Perhaps a pumpkin and potato potage... something that's easy on the throat...*mumble, mumble.*"

"Woof, woof. *(Hey, old man, I'm glad you're thinking up a new menu, but you're gonna trip if you don't look where you're going.)*"

Sure enough, he catches his foot on the step, flies out of the room, and lands on the floor.

I'm right there next to him, not to help but to deliver an "I told you so."

I just wanted to cool off! It's your fault for expecting anything from this no-good hound!

"See you later, Routa. Don't make a ruckus and disturb the young lady's sleep."

"Woof! *(Okay!)*"

He returns to the kitchen, and I go outside to the shade of a tree and gaze up at the sky.

I really had no idea my lady was sick.

I did think it was strange they would build such a stately mansion out here in the middle of nowhere, but I didn't even consider that it might be to help her recover from an illness.

They said it was an illness that came once a year, like clockwork. What a strange disease.

Maybe it's like hay fever? I really have no idea, though.

She looks completely healthy right now. She was even playing with me in the garden just a while ago. But once the fever comes, she'll be sick for a whole month and won't be able to study or learn at all. So that's why she studies so much every day. She's making up for lost time. That's rough.

Lady Mary works so hard. Studying is difficult.

I'm not sorry I never have to study again.

I'm happy living my life as a pampered pooch.

"Mrow. *(Oh my, so this is where you were. I was looking all over for you.)*"

I hear a cat's voice close by as I'm resting in the shade of a tree.

I open one eye and look up to see a crimson cat with a basket in her mouth.

"Woof. *(Oh, Hecate? I thought you were having tea with Papa.)*"

"Mrroow? *(I am. Why?)*"

"Woof. *(Huh? But you're here right now.)*"

What's she talking about?

Is she slow?

"Mrrow. *(Here, just like I promised. I brought you some dessert.)*"

"Woof… *(Oh. Ohhh, now that you mention it…)*"

So she came to fulfill the promise she made before.

Hecate's so nice.

It must be in that basket.

"Mrrow. *(Wait just a minute. I'll get everything ready.)*"

She drops the basket and meows once. A cloth covering the contents of the basket flies up by itself and unfolds before me. Then a plate comes out, settling itself on top of the cloth. Tea that's just the right temperature pours itself into a cup. And so the spread continues setting itself.

"Woof! *(Wow, that's incredible!)*"

I'm sorry I called you a self-proclaimed witch.

It's as if the crockery itself is imbued with life.

"Mrrow. *(It's much too soon to be amazed.)*"

The next item to appear from the basket is a large circular pie. The crust on top has a basket weave design and has been baked to a golden brown. I can tell it's crispy just from looking at it, and the smell of butter drifts into my nose.

My stomach ignores the fact that I had a massive lunch earlier and begins to growl.

"Mrrow. *(We're just getting started.)*"

A floating knife slices the pie. The moment it cuts into the flaky pastry, the bright red contents ooze out.

"Woof? *(Are those raspberries?)*"

Raspberries are smaller than strawberries and just a little tart.

So this is what's going to compete with the old man's quiche.

"Mrow. *(Tee-hee. And the finishing touches.)*"

The last items to appear are a glass bottle and an egg. The bottle is filled with white liquid. The egg is cracked open, and the contents get added to the liquid.

As I wonder where this is going, the egg and liquid start mixing together. At the same time, the bottle freezes from the bottom up.

"Arwf?! *(What is that?! What is it?!)*"

"Mrow. *(It's fresh cream. You freeze it as it's being whipped.)*"

She's talking about ice cream! No—soft serve!

The velvety, cold confection garnishes a slice of pie.

Whoa! That looks so good!

"Mrow. *(Here you are.)*"

"Woof! *(Wow! Thank you!)*"

I bite into the pie with a *chomp*.

The pastry far surpasses the old man's quiche. The rich creaminess transforms the acidity of the raspberries into a strong, sweet flavor. This freshly made ice cream is delicious. Maybe because it was so vigorously whipped? It melts the moment it enters my mouth and spills across the entirety of my tongue.

The crispy pastry. The tart raspberries. The sweet ice cream.

These three sensations together bombard my senses.

What an incredible impact. I've never tasted a dessert this delicious before, not even in the old world.

"Mrrow? *(So? Does this make up for it?)*"

"Woof, woof! *(It's even better! This is amazing, Hecate! It's sooo good! Thanks!)*"

"Mrow. *(Tee-hee. You're welcome. I'm happy you like it so much.)*"

"Woof, woof! *(Hey, let's have it together! Oh, right. Lady Mary and the others should try this, too.)*"

My lady loves sweet things.

It would be a shame to eat this whole pie by myself.

"Meow. *(Don't worry. I made sure to make enough for everyone. I just went ahead and gave you yours first.)*"

Score! She said the magic words.

And she made enough for everyone? She doesn't miss a thing.

Hecate's neither a suspicious, sexy lady nor a gluttonous witch. She's a woman who has it together.

"Mrow. *(Just make sure you share some pie with this little lady as well.)*"

"Woof? *(This little lady?)*"

Who is she talking about?

The only other creature I can see is Hecate's crimson cat form.

"Mrow. *(Tee-hee. I told you already. I'm not a cat.)*"

She narrows her suspicious jade-colored eyes, then falls asleep right there.

"Bark! *(Whoa! Hey, are you all right? Are you tired? One of those people who gets exhausted easily?)*"

I'm really worried because there was no warning.

I prod the crimson cat's head with my nose, and she opens her eyes again.

"Mewl? *(Hmm, has the mistress finished her business?)*"

The crimson cat reaches out with her front paws and stretches.

She sounds different.

"W-woof? *(H-hey. What was that about?)*"

"Mwl? *(Excuse me?)*"

Our eyes meet.

"Mw-mw… *(Ah…ah…)*"

"Arf? *(Really, what's gotten into you?)*"

"Screeeeeeeee! *(N-nooooooo!!! Don't kill me! Don't eat me! D-don't violate meeeeeeee!!!)*"

Whaaaat?! Why would I do that?! What a horrible thing to say!

But before I can say anything, the crimson cat darts away in a straight line.

"Woof… *(What the…? Well, it'd be a shame to let the pie go to waste. Guess I'll eat it by myself!)*"

Completely ignoring the cat that fled, I dig into the rest of the pie.

† † †

"Mwl… *(Please excuse my rudeness earlier.)*"

The crimson cat returns just as I'm finishing off the pie.

"Woof. *(Oh, you're late. I've already eaten most of it. There's one bite left. Would you like it?)*"

"Mewl. *(Oh, no thank you. Please do not mind me. I always have to clean up—I mean, taste the trial bakes.)*"

"Woof. *(Really? More for me, then.)*"

I fill my mouth with the last of the ice-cream-covered pie.

Om-nom-nom.

Mmm, that was good to the last bite.

I lick the remaining ice cream from around my mouth and revel in the aftertaste.

The crimson cat waits patiently for me.

"Woof? *(So? Who are you? You're not Hecate, are you?)*"

Even I could tell. It was so obvious.

Her eyes are blue, and she talks differently. And the way she reacted the moment she saw me was weird.

"Mewl. *(Please forgive me. I am the top familiar of the witch of Felt-belk Forest, Nahura…meow.)*"

Why did she add an extra "meow" at the end?

"Mewl. *(Oh, my mistress keeps saying I don't sound like a cat. I thought it would be best to act more like one.)*"

You're clearly a cat just by looking at you.

Tacking on "meow" to the end of her sentence just sounds weird. That's strange. Maybe she's just worried about her character?

"Woof, woof. *(I don't think you need to worry about it that much. I'm Routa, by the way. It's nice to meet you, Nahura.)*"

"Mewl. *(It is a pleasure to make you acquaintance, Mr. Routa.)*"

"Woof. *(You don't need to call me 'mister.' Just Routa's fine.)*"

I have enough formalities with Garo and the other wolves.

"Mewl. *(Very well, Routa. Also, please excuse how rude I was before. I was surprised when I saw you right in front of me…)*"

"Woof. *(It's fine. Don't worry about it.)*"

This may be my face, but even I get a little scared seeing it in the mirror. To be honest, my face is way scarier than Garo's. I have no idea how everyone at the mansion is fine with me.

"Woof, woof? *(Anyway. How are you different from a normal cat?)*"

She said she was a familiar, but does that mean there's a difference?

"Mewl. *(Oh yes. I am a homunculus created by my mistress, meow. Although she did use a real cat's corpse as a vessel, so I am a bit different from a true homunculus.)*"

"Woof. *(A homunculus! That's sounds like real fantasy.)*"

Seeing Hecate's magic firsthand definitely reaffirmed the fact that I've come to another world.

"Woof? *(So what exactly is the difference?)*"

"Mewl. *(Hmm, let me think. I am much smarter than a regular cat, I can use a little magic, and I can become my mistress's eyes and ears. Oh, and I won't die even if my head comes off.)*"

"Arwf?! *(Th-that's terrifying! What the hell?! That's so creepy!)*"

"Mew. *(Would you like to see? There will be a lot of blood, so I don't really recommend it.)*"

"Woof! Woof! *(No thank you! You're way scarier than my face!)*"

"Mewl. *(Oh, really? I think your face is considerably more horrifying.)*"

"Woof, woof! *(Ha-ha-ha! You cheeky cat!)*"

I'll let that one slide.

"Mewl. *(You are just as my mistress said you would be, meow.)*"

"Arwf? *(Huh? What did she say?)*"

"Mew. *(That you are as kind as your face is terrifying. She is thrilled she made friends with you. Even at her age, she is full of vitality and has started making sweets. I have never seen her like this before.)*"

"W-woof…? *(Sh-she said my face is scary, huh…?)*"

That might be a problem.

I'm worried everyone here at the mansion will find out what I really am and chase me out.

"Mewl. *(She is always in high spirits when she leaves. It is almost sickening, meow. It is most unbecoming at her age. Most unbecoming.)*"

"*What* is most unbecoming at *whose* age?"

A shadow had crept up behind Nahura as she spoke.

"G-gmew?! *(M-mistress?! When did you get here?!)*"

"Just now. You forget that I can hear everything you say, no matter where you are."

"Mewwwww! *(N-no! That's a violation of my feline rights, meow! Even a familiar needs her privacy, meow!)*"

"Silence. There is no such thing as privacy for a familiar who makes careless remarks about her master."

"Meeeow! *(P-please don't punish meeeeeeee!)*"

Hecate lifts Nahura in the air with her magic and flips her upside down. Hecate looks at her with a sadistic smile while the pie plate, cloth, and other cutlery put themselves away.

"Let's see. How shall I punish you today?"

"Meeeow! *(Noooo!! Don't put me in any strange monster bodies!)*"

Does she normally do that…?

I cannot do anything.

I am just a regular dog, after all. Good-bye, Nahura. I barely knew thee.

"Your sentence is punishment by bath."

Wh-what in the world is punishment by bath? What kind of torture is that code for?

"Hsss! Hsss! *(Noooo! Not a bath!)*"

"You haven't had a bath for three days. If you're going to be my familiar, then you're going to be clean and tidy."

Oh. It's just a normal bath.

† † †

"Woof. *(So now we're all having a bath.)*"

I think back over everything that just happened!

This mansion is equipped with three baths of various sizes, and we are at the largest. It's so large that ten people could fit in all at once.

Of course, we don't normally use it, but since Hecate's here, it's been run specially for her.

The damp scent of steam really ups the mood for a bath.

Bathing is one of Japan's top three pleasures in life! The other two are a cold beer after a bath and baseball tournaments!

Wow, I sound like an old man...

"It's been a while since you've had one of your beloved baths, right, Routa?"

"Woof! Woof! *(Yep! I'm even happy with just swimming!)*"

"Hee-hee-hee. Let's have a race!"

My stark-naked lady heads straight for the tub.

"Ah, please wait, my lady! Be careful not to slip!"

Chasing after her is the panicky maid with a towel wrapped around her.

"Accept your punishment, Nahura. I've already told you I would clean every nook and cranny."

"Meeeow! *(Forgive me! Please forgive me, mistress!)*"

Hecate really lives up to the name of an erotic—I mean elf—with her voluptuous body shamelessly exposed as she takes Nahura to the bath.

"Watch it—there's someone behind you. Get a move on."

And behind me is Zenobia.

It's refreshing to see her burning bronze hair tied up. She looks like a knight with her toned body, but her full breasts are as large as Hecate's.

Well, this is a sight to see.

If I were still human, I probably would have gotten a nosebleed and fainted.

But I'm just a cute little puppy, so I can be forgiven. Heh-heh-heh.

"Hey. I dare you to try anything funny with the lady. Then I'll be permitted to wring your neck."

A chilling voice whispers in my ear.

Ha-ha-ha. Zenobia's murderous intent is really something today.

…I think I'm going to cry.

† † †

"You're so fast, Routa!"

"Woof, woof! *(Ha-ha-ha! Here goes the high-speed pup!)*"

My lady has her arms around my neck as I swim around the bath.

"Amazing! Ha-ha-ha-ha-ha-ha!"

"Woof! Woof! *(Mwa-ha-ha! I won't be beaten by any old amusement park ride!!)*"

I'll give it everything I've got to make sure Lady Mary is having fun.

That's all this mutt needs to worry about.

"Phew. We've built up a good sweat. I think it's time we had a little more fun."

Hecate is sitting in a lounge chair, her skin white as an egg, slippery with droplets.

A bucket of ice had been left next to the bath.

"Hey, Nahura. Don't just lie there; come and help us."

"M-mewww… *(I—I can't…)*"

Nahura, who had been thoroughly cleaned, is now stretched out like grilled mochi by Hecate's feet.

"You are hopeless. Zenobia, come over here."

"Y-yes! How can I help?"

Zenobia practically leaps out of the bath when called.

Whoa, even Zenobia bows and scrapes around Hecate.

She nervously walks over to Hecate, marching like a rookie soldier, and stands in front of her.

"That won't do at all. Come here. Care to have a drink with me?"

She pats the lounge chair next to her and extracts a bottle from the ice bucket.

"What?! That's the master's prized wine…! That's the sovereign seal of Rome, distilled only once every hundred years, made in 1685…!"

"Hee-hee. And I brought it with me."

Hecate strokes the bottle as if caressing a lover's cheek.

"B-brought it with you? And you don't see anything wrong with—?!"

"Don't worry so much."

Don't worry, you say?

That's the wine Papa's always cherished and kept safe. I've seen it under lock and key in the wine cellar. I heard it costs more than a house…

"Gandolf won't get angry about something like this."

"No, but well, you know……!"

That's true. He won't get angry. He'll just cry to himself all through the night. Poor Papa.

"Now, now, come on then."

Zenobia shrinks back as Hecate pulls the cork out of the wine bottle. She pours the ruby liquid into two glasses.

"Ah! Ah! It's going to overflow…!"

"Cheers!"

With a *ting*, Hecate tilts her glass.

"Mmm, delicious. Come on, Zenobia—drink up. If anyone says anything, you can just tell them I forced you to do it."

"O-okay... Please excuse me."

To refuse now would be rude, and the crime has already been committed.

Zenobia steels herself and takes a sip.

"Th-this is...! What a rich flavor...!"

Her eyes snap open, and she stares at the glass.

"It has the strong fragrance of summer flowers, but upon swallowing, it's so cool it's like an icicle slipping down your throat. There is a decadent richness that spreads across your tongue and a bitterness that hits your nose...!"

What are you, a sommelier?

Thank you for the wonderfully poetic review. Very nice. I want to try some, too.

"Hey! Where are you going, Routa?"

I pull away from Lady Mary's arms wrapped around my neck, get out of the bath, and head for Hecate.

"Oh my, I had a feeling you would come. Gandolf told me you knew your liquor, Routa."

Tch, she saw this coming?

At least it's right to the point.

"Woof! Woof! *(Please let me have some! Just a taste of that wine that could buy ten of me!)*"

"Hee-hee. I don't know—should I?"

"Woof?! Woof?! *(Shall I show you my tummy?! Shall I bark three times for you?!)*"

"That doesn't sound fun at all."

Hecate thinks for a little while, then a familiar cheeky grin appears on her face.

"Hee-hee-hee......"

She tilts her glass and pours some wine onto her arm. The ruby liquid dribbles down onto her hand and drips off her fingertips.

"Here you go."

"Grr…woof! *(Y-you—! Are you making fun of me?! Who do you think I am?! Do you really think I'd lick it off you?!)*"

Because you'd be right! Thanks for the wine!

Lick. Lick.

This is a fitting reward for one of my station.

Lick. Lick. Lick.

"Arf! *(Whoa, this is* so *good…!)*"

It's just as Zenobia raved.

"Some more, perhaps?"

Hecate recrosses her alluring legs, chuckling sadistically.

Whoa, that's a nice smile. She looks completely sadistic. What a witch.

I lick her! I lick her fingers until they become soaked!

"Hmph…"

Lady Mary seems upset about this.

Aw, crap. I've put her in a bad mood.

But I also can't pull myself away from this wine!

I'm completely engrossed in S&M play with a witch!

Lick! Lick!

"It's not fair that Routa gets some. I want some wine, too."

So that's what she's upset about.

"This wine is a little too strong for you, Mary. And seeing as your illness is almost upon us, I've prepared this instead."

Saying that, Hecate reaches into the ice bucket and takes out a small bottle filled with peach-colored liquid.

On closer inspection, I see a number of flowers have sunk to the bottom of the bottle.

"This is syrup I made with my own roses. It smells quite wonderful. Please try some."

She quietly pours a little of the thick pink syrup into some chilled water. A single rose comes out, creating a beautiful drink with a gradation of colors.

"Wow, it's so pretty… And it smells amazing."

"Doesn't it? It's also good for beauty. It's all yours."

Hecate prompts Lady Mary with the glass, and she drinks it in one go.

The moment she finishes, her cheeks, rosy from the bath, spread into a wide grin.

"Mmm! It's so sweet! But also refreshing! Thank you, Doctor!"

"You're welcome. Would you like some, too, Miranda? No one will mind if you have a little bit?"

Hecate calls out to the maid, who's standing back.

Well, Zenobia's a freeloader, but the maid's working right now. You shouldn't let her drink alcohol.

"Thank you very much, Lady Hecate."

She gingerly accepts the chilled rose water.

I've finally learned the maid's name. Miranda.

Lady Mary sits on a lounge chair. With drinks in hand, the ladies begin chatting happily, accompanied by a dog that eagerly licks the witch's fingers and a cat stretched out on the floor like grilled mochi.

† † †

Five days have passed since the bath, and just as Hecate predicted, Lady Mary's fever hits.

The illness is much more serious than I'd previously thought.

Everyone has been in such high spirits that I underestimated it and thought it wouldn't be a big deal.

That was a huge misunderstanding.

Everyone is in Lady Mary's room watching over her. The sun is already half-set, spilling orange light into the room.

Her condition has been getting worse since the morning. She can't even stand anymore and lies on the bed, her breath ragged.

Ice packs have been placed on her head and armpits to cool her down, but her condition does not look good.

"Did you make sure she took the medicine properly?"

Hecate check's Lady Mary's pulse.

"Yes. The correct amount after every meal."

Miranda the maid nods.

"Okay. If the fever gets any worse, then you should increase this medicine, too."

She takes a bottle of red liquid out of her bag and pours it into a little glass.

"Can you sit up, Mary?"

"...Yes, Dr. Hecate..."

As she tries to pull the top half of her shaking body up, a large hand moves to support her back.

"Thank you, Father..."

"There, now; take it slow."

Lady Mary sits up as Papa supports her.

I don't know if her throat is inflamed, but she looks like she's in pain as she drinks a little bit of the medicine.

"Cough...cough..."

"Good girl. Lie down now. The medicine should soon take effect."

She's helped back down, and the ice pack returns to her head.

"Arww, arww...? *(Are you okay, my lady...?)*"

My tail refuses to wag as I shuffle closer to her.

Everyone looks like they've seen this all before, so I didn't think it would be this bad. But she's really suffering.

Even when I had the flu, I was never this bad.

I huff through my nose, and Lady Mary lays her tiny hand on top of my head.

She always looks so happy, but right now, she's just weak.

"I'll be fine, Routa... I'll get better soon... Then we can play at the lake together again... Dr. Hecate can come with us, too..."

I wonder if it's because of the fever, but her voice sounds incredibly faint, too.

"Oh my, I would love that. I will have to make some more dessert to take with us."

"Heh-heh... I'm really looking forward to your desserts..."

Lady Mary smiles briefly as if Hecate just said something amusing; then her hand slips off my head.

"Arww! *(M-my lady!)*"

"Calm down. It's just the medicine making her sleep."

Hecate quickly whispers in my ear as she puts Lady Mary's arm back under the covers.

She doesn't seem surprised by this at all.

"I think her fever should go down soon; then you should make sure she eats and takes her medicine while she has energy. Make sure she drinks plenty of water, too. She'll likely feel worse when she wakes up, so wipe away any sweat. This red medicine is strong, so give it to her no more than twice a day, with at least six hours between each dose."

"I understand. I shall do as you have asked."

Hecate gives the instructions in quick succession, and Miranda respectfully bows.

"D-Dr. Hecate! W-will my daughter be all right?! Is her condition worse than last year?!"

Papa begs Hecate. He looks like he's in even more pain than Lady Mary when he looks at her sleeping face.

"Please keep it down, Gandolf. We have a sick patient present. Your body may have grown, but you haven't changed a bit. You're crying into your wonderful beard."

"*Sob.* But…but……"

"Everything will be fine. As long as she remains stable, she will be better within a month. You know this. It's the same every year."

"Y-yes…"

The dignified image I had of Papa just keeps falling in my eyes. Seeing him like this, I can tell how hard this is hitting him.

Well, fathers all over the world get like this over their daughters.

I'll just pretend I didn't see it.

Which makes me wonder, how old *is* Hecate?

It seems like she's known Papa since he was young, which means she must be a *lot* older than she looks.

I guess this is pretty normal for an elf.

"Routa?"

Eek! Hecate's smiling at me!

Her wordless smile is terrifying!

"Arww, arww? *(H-hey, Hecate? There's something I want to discuss with you. Do you have a minute?)*"

It's not that I want to change the subject. I really do have something I want to ask her.

"…Please excuse me for a moment. You should step out for a bit yourself, Gandolf, and get some rest."

She seems to have guessed what I'm feeling and rises from her chair.

I casually follow her.

† † †

We leave the mansion where there may be prying eyes and sit in the shade of a tree.

I look up at the evening sunset. The breeze blowing in from the violet sky seems lonely, and the cold night air is starting to creep in.

"What did you want to talk about? Although I already know what you're going to say."

"Woof, woof. *(Um, well, you know. You're an amazing witch, Hecate, and I can tell you're an amazing doctor, too. Even a newbie like me can tell. And I know this is rude of me to ask, but…)*"

"You want me to hasten Mary's recovery, even if only a little?"

She tilts her head and stares at me as she finishes my sentence.

"Woof… *(Yes…)*"

Then again, if there was a way to do that, she would have already.

Even I think it's a stupid question.

But I had to ask.

I know there's no way to help; I shouldn't have asked.

I had to try for Lady Mary's sake, though. Guess I can't judge Papa for getting emotional.

"Woof, woof. *(Sorry. That's a stupid request. Just forget about it. There's no way there'd be anything that could help that easily.)*"

"There is."

"Arf?! *(There is? Wait. There is?!)*"

I'm so surprised I ask her twice.

"I'll explain the steps you need to take."

She takes out her wand and draws in the air with it. Light hangs where she traces, creating marks as if she were scribbling on the ground.

"The medicine I'm using now is a makeshift solution. It specializes in maintaining stamina and reducing the fever, but it has no effect on the cause of the illness."

"Woof... *(Hmm, I see...)*"

"The disease breaks out for about a month, but I have no way to treat the root of the problem... No way on hand, at least."

"Woof? *(Hmm? So there's a way?)*"

"Yes. The medicine I make is very effective, but a lot of the ingredients I use are incredibly common."

So if she can get better ingredients, then the medicine will work better, too.

"Wyrmnil."

"Woof? *(Wyrmnil?)*"

"It's a mystical medicinal herb that only grows in dragons' dens. I've only been able to get my hands on it twice. It had deteriorated in the dry climate, making the medicine less effective. But even then, I was able to create a wonderful miracle medicine with it."

"Woof, woof... *(Then you just need to ask Papa...)*"

The family is incredibly wealthy. If she tells Papa about this, then he'll definitely get his hands on it.

"This is not something you can buy from any market. It has been a long time since I met an adventurer who could stand against the might of a dragon. Even if I make requests to the guild, it is still a difficult plant to get hold of. Dragons are a rare species, making it impossible to find their nests. You're more likely to find fakes out in the market."

"Woof… *(Aghh…)*"

Dragons.

Those are strong, right?

And she said she doesn't know where any are.

"Howeeeever."

"Arw? *(However?)*"

"In ancient times, people were too afraid to invade the center of this expansive forest for fear of a rare dragon that dwelled within."

She's playing innocent while poking her index finger into her cheek for added effect.

"…Arww? *(So you're saying I should go look for it?)*"

"Tee-hee. That would be impossible for an ordinary dog. For an *ordinary* dog, that is."

She smiles suggestively and tickles my ear alluringly.

"I should be getting back now. What you do with this information is up to you. But do not worry, for Mary will be better in a month. I can guarantee that."

She stands up, brushes some leaves off her knees, then turns around and walks off.

"…Arf… *(Hmm…)*"

I think alone in the shadow of the tree.

My goal has always been to live a pet life as a good-for-nothing pup.

I refuse to do anything dangerous, or scary, or painful. I outright refuse to do any work.

No corporate slavery. No manual labor.

Eat delicious food every single day, sleep as much as I want, and get hugs all the time.

That's all.

That really is everything.

"… *(That's why…)*"

I have no reason whatsoever to look for it.

But seeing my lady suffering is not an enjoyable pet life at all.

I can only live my life as a good-for-nothing pup because Lady Mary is with me.

"Woof! *(I'll just go and come right back! Until then, my comfortable house, adieu!)*"

Oh, don't get me wrong.

This isn't for Lady Mary. It's to protect my way of life.

After leaving the mansion, the first thing I do upon entering the forest is...

"Awoooooooooooooooooooo!! *(Garooooooooemon! I need your heeeeeeeelp!!)*"

...call for help.

I call Garo from the cliff that I stood on when I first howled at the moon.

Pfft. Laugh at me if you want. It's totally like me to rely on others to get what I need.

And besides, I have no clue where to find a dragon's nest or what wyrmnil even looks like. From how Hecate went on about it, I'm guessing I'll know it when I see it.

"Grwl. *(At your service, my king.)*"

She soon appears after hearing my howl.

"Woof! *(Garoemon!)*"

"Grwl. *(Yes, my king! ...Er, 'emon'? Forgive me, my king. What does 'emon' mean?)*"

"Woof. *(Oh, it's nothing.)*"

I really wanted someone to say something like, "Aw, Routa, you're so helpless. What's wrong? Did Zenobia whale on ya again?"

I guess I'm asking for a bit too much.

"Woof. *(Anyway, why are you standing all the way over there? Come here.)*"

Usually when she pops up out of nowhere, she appears right next to me, but this time she was far enough away that I wasn't sure she could even hear me.

"Grw... *(O-okay. No, wait— But...)*"

Is she still worried about me saying her face was scary?

Sorry I was being so honest. I thought you were a guy.

I really can't tell the sex of a wolf just by looking at it.

"Woof. *(Sorry. I take back everything I said before. My face is much more terrifying. I'm truly sorry.)*"

"Grwl. *(N-no! Your eminence's face is most glorious! I-it's...w-w-w-wonderful...)*"

It doesn't matter how bashful you sound. I'm not suddenly going to swoon over you.

I'm really not a furry, after all.

But you are incredibly fluffy. As someone else who's fluffy, I am quite jealous.

"Grw. *(So, my king. How may I assist you today? ... Wait! Do you finally want to invade the human—?)*"

"Woof... *(No, just drop that already...)*"

She really wants to get rid of the humans.

That's just the kind of provocation Zenobia's waiting for.

"Woof. *(I wanted to ask you about something.)*"

"Grw! *(Yes, whatever you need!)*"

"Bark? *(Do you know where I can find a dragon's nest?)*"

Garo and the wolves watch over every nook and cranny of this forest. They probably know if there's a dragon here.

That's why I called her.

I can't just wander around the forest aimlessly. That's too much work.

"Grw... *(A dragon...)*"

Garo thinks for a while before her head snaps up as if she thought of something.

"Grw. *(I have never seen one myself, but I did hear a story about one from my mother.)*"

Ooh, I'm glad I asked Garo. Looks like she has an idea where one might live.

Garo points her nose north. I can just barely see the faint shadows of mountains against the cloudy night sky.

"Grwl, grwl. *(You can see them, right? Just north of the forest, at the foot of the sacred mountains, a blue dragon sleeps behind a waterfall. My mother told me this as a bedtime story.)*"

"Woof. *(Yikes. That's really far away.)*"

"Grw. *(Yes, it is. It would take us three days to get there. It would possibly take you half the time, my king.)*"

Don't be ridiculous.

I ignore her outrageous assumption. The only way to know for sure is to go.

"Bark. *(All right, no time like the present. I'll be off, then.)*"

"Grwl! *(Then I shall accompany you! It would be an honor to hunt a dragon with you! Please grant me this privilege!)*"

"Woof. *(No, no, no. I'm not going hunting, okay? I'm going to sneak in and steal some wyrmnil. Got it?)*"

Just imagine the dragon finding me sneaking into its nest. A dragon so strong, there's nothing you can do against it. No way to look cool at that point. If I were found, I'd just have to turn tail and run. All I could do is run. And if I have to run, it's best if I'm alone.

"Grwl! *(But it's dangerous to go alone…!)*"

"Woof, woof. *(Don't worry. I'll be in and out lickety-split. You can just wait here.)*"

"Grw… *(…P-please forgive me. It was rude of me to oppose your will. Unforgivable…!)*"

She grovels on the ground in apology.

Uh-oh. I may have overdone it with the "Silence, whelp" thing.

Just as I'm at a loss over what to do with Garo, I hear the crunch of someone stepping on the stones behind me.

"Grwl?! *(Wh-who's there?!)*"

Garo instantly leaps forward to protect my back.

"Grwwl...?! *(What are you?! How could you have gotten so close without me knowing......?!)*"

"Arwf? *(Huh?)*"

The way she asks that catches my ear, and I spin around.

"Y-you... You're secretly meeting monsters in the dead of night......?!"

There stands the knight, Zenobia.

"A-arf! *(A-ahhh, crap! She's the last person I wanted to find out about this!)*"

This is bad!

This is the worst situation ever!

Zenobia is the least oblivious person in the mansion, and now she's seen me with Garo.

"Grrrr...! *(Human...! Don't you dare take another step toward the king!)*"

She wrinkles her nose and bares her teeth.

Whoa! Whoa! Hold it! Wait, Garo! Your threat's going to have the opposite effect!

"That giant form and murderous intent...! You're not just any wolf...! I thought you were suspicious, but you're actually—!"

Uh-oh. This is an explosive situation between Garo and Zenobia.

This is going to end in a bloodbath.

Everything's fine. I can fix this. I actually devised a plan just in case this ever happened.

I was worried the day would come when my identity would be discovered, so I've been practicing diligently. I failed a lot, but through trial and error, I managed to work out a great killer technique. It's unmistakably my strongest killer technique to date.

And now is the time to reveal it.

"Arwf! *(Let's do this!)*"

I quickly lower my head and roll forward.

Their glares move to me.

I remain lying on my back, loll out my tongue in a cute way, and start panting like an excited pup.

"Haah-haah-haah-haah! *(Killer technique: submission pose!)*"

Let me explain.

Submission pose is a technique dogs have used since ancient times as a sign of ultimate fealty toward humans while also letting them know there are no enemies nearby, executed by exposing their vulnerable midsection, causing weak-minded humans to drop their guards and approach the irresistibly fluffy body of the dog until they give in to the urge to pet them. *(Deep breath.)*

"You…you still think such cute behavior will work on me…?!"

"Haah-haah-haah-haah! *(Mwa-ha-ha-ha-ha! You cannot kill me! You can't even try! Even a proud knight like you is defenseless, right?! Riiiight?! For shame! You will be embarrassed till the end of your days if you try to cut me down now! Riiiight?! Right?! Riiiight?!)*"

"U-urgn…!"

"Haah-haah-haah-haah! *(Mwa-ha-ha-ha-ha-ha! I love your frustrated expression!)*"

I really want to lick her.

"Grwl… *(Wh-what is that pose, oh king…?! One as lowly as I could not possibly fathom what the great king is doing at present…!)*"

"Woof, woof! *(Garo! What are you doing?! Hurry up and get with the program!)*"

"Grwl?! *(Wh-what?! Me?!)*"

"Bark! Bark! *(Of course! Come on! Hurry up! Do it now!)*"

"Grr… *(B-but it's so… No, I swore I would be loyal to the king. No matter what order he may give me, I shall humbly accept it as his imperial guard! Everything my king does is righteous!)*"

Garo flashes Zenobia a glare, then does exactly as I did, exposing her tummy.

"Haah-haah-haah-haah! *(This may be an order from my king, but it's still a disgrace…! Tch. I'll kill you! I'll kill you, human!)*"

"Haah-haah-haah-haah! *(Good! But not good enough! More*

cuteness! Tilt your front paws and really sell it! That's it! That's good! Now look! She's going to give in any moment now! We've almost won!)"

The two of us Fen Wolves convey with all our might that we're not Zenobia's enemies as her eyes spin.

"Ugg…grk…ghn. All right, fine! Stop it! I surrender!"

Zenobia finally gives in and falls to her knees.

Phew. We won.

That was easy.

"Grw… *(What my king did was certainly effective… But is it all right like this…?)*"

Garo seems to be suffering from the bottom of her heart as she mumbles.

Of course it's all right. We won without spilling a single drop of blood.

My pride as Fenrir, King of the Fen Wolves? I don't care about that. The only thing I want to do is live my life as a pampered pooch.

Oh, I feel like I just said something really cool.

"…I won't ask you what you truly are for now."

Zenobia takes a deep breath and looks directly at me.

"……Hey. Can you stop that now? I'm trying to have a serious conversation."

Oh, whoops.

We roll back over and sit down with our backs straight.

"I overheard what Lady Hecate said to you."

Hey, now… Eavesdropping is not an admirable thing to do.

At least, I'd normally give a jab like that, but I couldn't dismiss her sober expression.

"I want to help the young lady, too. So you're after wyrmnil, are you? I'm going with you to get it."

"Grwl! *(No way! I will not allow a human like you to guard the king!)*"

"Woof, woof. *(Stop it. Garo, sit. Sit, girl. Siiiit. Doooown!)*"

"Arwn… *(As you command, my king…)*"

She was about to bare her teeth again but stopped.

"You asked this black beast about the dragon's nest, didn't you? I'm guessing it's at the foot of the sacred mountains."

Wow, she's sharp.

It's like she's a different person from the one who keeps picking up fake swords.

"Do not worry. I have already prepared everything."

She certainly does seem well prepared with travel clothes and cloak, a bag on her shoulder that smells like it has food in it, and a giant steel case on her back. She's certainly better off than me, who left with nothing but the fur on his back. She has it all.

Looks like it'll be impossible to convince her otherwise. Not that she'd understand what I'm saying either way.

"We should hurry. The sooner we do this, the sooner the lady's illness will be cured."

Then she runs off.

"Woof. (Oh, in that case, you'll have to stay here, Garo. I would really appreciate it if you protect the mansion while I'm away.)"

"Grw. (As you command. I, Garo, shall protect your home with my life. Please be safe.)"

I leave Garo with her head bowed low and chase after Zenobia.

Wait up, Zenobia!

That's not north!

† † †

Dirt flies up as my four paws dig into the ground.

I take the lead, racing through the dark forest.

I glance behind me to see Zenobia easily keeping up.

The canopy blocks out the moonlight, so there isn't a single source of light in the pitch-black woods. The ground is uneven because of the mulchy soil and exposed roots. If it weren't for my wolflike body, I wouldn't be able to traverse this area at all.

Yet, Zenobia is running through the forest as if she's traveling along a road.

"Hey, stop looking back. You needn't concern yourself with me. You should focus on the goal ahead," she says without needing to catch her breath.

Just you watch.

She said all that with a straight face, yet she was the one who went the wrong way just now.

She usually acts like she's got her head on backward, so I was sure she'd struggle. She's in rare form today, though. I didn't think she'd be able to keep up with me.

The giant metallic case on her back looks incredibly heavy, but she's so strong that it appears weightless.

It also seems like she can see clearly through the dark forest.

So she has amazing eyesight and good legs.

Looks like I can probably pick up the pace a little more.

I bark once and run a little faster.

"Hmph, what's this? Is that all you've got? I have a lot more energy left, you know."

Zenobia scoffs through her nose.

Oh, really? Do you really?

Little Zenobia wants me to turn it up?

Bring it on! I'll make you cry!

"Woof! Woof! *(Here it comes! I'll show you just how fast I can* really *run!)*"

Grrrr.

Like a bolt of lightning, I weave through the gaps in the trees.

"Tch. Not bad! But I won't lose!"

Her face scrunches slightly as she matches my gait.

No way! I thought I was running with everything I had!

She's carrying gear and only has two legs! How is she able to keep up?!

Whoa, Zenobia's really something.

What an amazing physique.

If she hadn't used fake swords that snapped in half, she might have actually killed me…

U-uh-oh… If she manages to get a sword that's not a piece of crap, she might actually succeed…!

I'd better come up with another cute killer technique soon…!

I set off at a violent dash to try and get away from her.

† † †

"*Wheeze…wheeze……*"

"Haff…haff…"

Th-that's it. I'm done.

I can't run anymore…

Zenobia and I stagger out of the forest and collapse on the bank of a beautiful brook.

"N-not bad…"

"W-woof… (*I didn't think you'd keep up till the end… Looks like I underestimated you…*)"

I remain lying on my front as I look up at the sky to see the day is already starting to break.

So that means it's about three…maybe four in the morning…?

If it was evening when we left the mansion, that means we were running for close to ten hours.

Ugh, I'm exhausted…

I wanna go home…

Come to think of it, how far did we go…?

We ran as hard as we could straight north, but I've lost all sense of distance.

"I can hear waterfalls. It's close."

Zenobia already has her breath back and is looking north.

How could she have gotten her second wind faster than a Fen Wolf like me?

Upon perking my ears up, I can hear the rushing of a large waterfall. It sounds like it's a few kilometers away from us.

Garo said it would take three days to get here, but we arrived a lot faster than that.

"Let's have a quick rest, then enter the dragon's den. We need our bodies to be in perfect condition."

Zenobia finds a large, flat rock on the riverbank and puts her bag down.

I peek inside to see basic cooking equipment as well as a giant hunk of brown bread, a fist-sized lump of raclette cheese, and some smoked meat.

"*Sniff, sniff. (This smells like applewood chips. This is the smoked meat the old man made. That bastard. He had some hidden away somewhere...!)*"

There wasn't any of this left when I snuck into the kitchen for a snack.

Damn, he tricked me!

"Wh-what? I didn't take this without asking. I asked Master James, and he prepared it for me."

Zenobia shrinks from my glare.

Her flustered look is still super-cute. I really wanna lick her.

"Go look for some dry branches. I'll collect some water."

"Woof. *('Kaaay.)*"

We work together to get a fire and some food together.

† † †

The firewood burns red with a crackle.

"Woof! Woof! *(Food! Food! Faster! Faster!)*"

"Hold your horses. There's a way to make this even tastier, you know."

Zenobia slices the brown bread. The crust is as hard as stone, but when she turns it over, I can see that the center is surprisingly light and fluffy. Then she takes out the chunk of smoked meat and cuts it into thin slices with a knife before laying it across the bread.

"And finally..."

She stabs the tip of her knife into the cheese and positions it over the fire. The cheese emits a heavenly fragrance as it softens and begins losing shape. Once it melts and starts to bubble, she carefully lays it on top of the smoked meat. The cheese and meat become entangled as both seep into the fluffy bread.

"Arwf?! *(C-could this be…?!)*"

The dish I've only ever dreamed about when I was a kid, *tartine de savoie*…?!

It's not just the cheese but the meat that makes this look even more delicious!

"Here. You've waited long enough. Dig in."

Doing her best to sound indifferent, she offers me the food.

We don't have any plates, so she just places it on the ground.

She's such a *tsundere*. I really, really wanna lick her.

"I'm going to eat it all first if you're not having any."

"Woof, woof! *(Ah, I'll eat it! I'll eat it!)*"

I can almost taste the applewood used to smoke the meat that now rests beneath the gooey, melted raclette cheese. The two aromas combine in my nose, creating a smell as sweet as a bouquet of flowers.

"Woof! *(I can tell it's good even before having any! Time to dig in!)*"

I gratefully accept the *tartine de savoie* that Zenobia made with her own two hands.

"Hey, you don't have to inhale it. I was only joking when I said I would eat it all first. Can't you eat a bit more gracefully?"

The fragrance of the cheese, the umami of the smoked meat, and the sweetness of the bread, which gets stronger with every bite—all possess a simple yet refined flavor.

It's so incredibly delicious.

If this had been on the morning menu at the café when I was a corporate slave, I would have shown up to work every day with a smile on my face.

Ahhh, if only I could have started my days off with a meal this elegant!

What a bitter memory…

Forget about that world. I'm a happy pup now.

Zenobia checks to see that I'm eating my helping before she starts preparing her own.

She normally looks at me with such disdain, but now she's making sure I eat my food first. She really is a *tsundere*.

I am going to lick her someday.

I swear it.

† † †

"...The truth is...I know you don't have any ill intent."

It's a silent night under the starlit sky, with only the sound of a bubbling brook. Zenobia suddenly speaks up as we're drinking a rich fruit wine that's been cut with hot water. The fruit wine by itself doesn't have a lot of alcohol, so it's not quite enough to warm the body.

The fire dwindles, and a tree branch is thrown into the ashes, bringing it back to life.

I can see the side of Zenobia's bashful face in the light of the weak fire. She's lost all her usual fierceness and looks almost kind.

"You love the young lady dearly. I know that. But my instincts still tell me you're dangerous."

"Arww. *(I know you're trying to be serious, but your instincts are wrong.)*"

No matter how you look at me, I'm an adorable pet.

I'm just a little big, and my face is just a little scary.

Just close your eyes, and you'll see past it.

"The way your body does not tire is not ordinary. I cannot imagine how much more you will grow. I believe you will become a monster stronger than anything I've killed before."

She grits her teeth.

"You might be well-behaved now, but one day, you're going to turn back into a monster and hurt someone. That's what I'm afraid of. That one day you'll hurt the master, young lady, or someone at the mansion... And when that happens, I'll..."

She hugs her knees. Her fetal pose reminds me of an abandoned puppy.

"Those people accepted me like a part of their family. The only thing I can do is fight, and the only way I can repay them is with my sword. Which is why, even if they hate me, I'll dispose of y——!"

"Arwf! *(Good night!)*"

I use my front paws as a pillow and lie down.

"Ah! Hey! I'm trying to have a serious heart-to-heart here! Listen!"

"*Yaaaawn. (I don't care. My only lot in life is as a no-good, lazy dog. There will never be a day when your instincts are right, so there's no point listening.)*"

I yawn loudly and turn my face away from her.

Honestly, she looks like a human but acts like a stray dog. It's like someone just tossed her out and she's begging to be taken care of.

She's so sly. She really is the eternal adversary to my pet life.

I won't give up my place as the sole good-for-nothing in the family!

† † †

"It seems the day has come where I will wield this sword once more…"

As the morning sun peeks out over the horizon, we wake up from our brief nap and then prepare to set off again.

Well, a pup like me only has the fur on his back, so I have nothing to do as I watch Zenobia do all the work.

She opens the metal case that she left on the bank and retrieves what was stored inside.

I peek from behind her to see a giant blade and a long handle in her hands.

Are they stored separately? If she attaches the grip now, the whole thing will be taller than Zenobia.

The tip of the weapon is round and massive, almost *swollen*, and the blade itself is quite thick.

That thing is too big to be called a sword. Erected before me is a ridiculously huge hunk of metal.

How in the world is someone meant to wield it?

"This is a magic sword that has been passed down through the Lionheart family for generations. It is called Dragvein. My ancestor, the god of war Georg, used it to slay evil dragons."

The blade has dark, profound lines, resembling veins, running along the length of it.

If she told me it had been cursed by an evil dragon's blood, I'd have to believe her. Something about that sinister blade is seriously *off.*

"This sword will be most suitable for the coming battle. As the descendant of proud dragon slayers, I must claim the title of dragon slayer myself! This must be how the god of war felt!"

"Arf?! Arf?! *(That's completely wrong! Zenobia?! We're not here to fight anything! We're just going to sneak in and swipe the wyrmnil! This is a stealth mission, not a battle!)*"

Zenobia smiles slightly when I bark at her.

"I'm kidding. But we do have to prepare for the worst if we're discovered."

She checks that the blade and hilt are tightly fastened, then puts her tools back in the case.

Looking at it again, it really is much too big for any human to carry.

Just as I think this, she holds the ridiculously huge sword aloft.

"Arwf?! *(Wha—?!)*"

She shows no signs of fatigue as the blade glides effortlessly through the air.

"Arwf?! *(How can you hold it like it's so light?! That's not right! The laws of physics! It breaks the laws of physics!)*"

She swings the blade around like it's no more than a stick.

"That's no good. It's a bit heavy. I must be getting rusty."

"Woof, woof! *(But you made it look so light! You wielded it without any problems!)*"

Her powerful swings create gusts of wind and cause the rocks on the riverbank to tremble.

She spins the sword faster, whipping up a tornado-strength gale.

"The day I quit being an adventurer and began living in the Faulkses' manor, I planned on throwing this sword away."

Why didn't she throw it away that day?

It's such a dangerous weapon—the world's better off without it.

"But I just couldn't do it. It's a precious family heirloom, and I also felt that a day like today would come."

As her blade dance reaches its climax, the giant sword stops abruptly.

A moment later, a tremendous gust of wind swirls around us. My cheeks flap in the strong breeze.

This sword is dangerous. It's completely different from the brittle fake swords she had before.

This is a real monster-slaying weapon.

And the wielder of this weapon is even more dangerous.

"Hmph…"

She returns the sword to the scabbard on her back and looks down at me.

"A-arf?! *(Wh-why are you looking at me? …You don't want to try that on me, right?! You don't wanna do a thing like that, right?!)*"

You can't!

I'll die! The moment it strikes the top of my head, I'll actually die!

"…Let's go. I don't know where we're going, so I'm relying on you."

"A-arf! *(Y-yes, ma'am!)*"

Looks like I was worried over nothing.

I wonder what she's thinking as she stares at me before swiveling around and walking off.

Thank goodness. I thought she was going to murder me before the dragon did.

I give thanks that I managed to escape death and then go on to direct Zenobia, who has walked off in the wrong direction yet again.

† † †

We continue moving toward the sound of rushing water until our objective comes into view.

A giant waterfall cascades down the side of a steep cliff. We're a good distance away from it, but the water spray still hits our faces. I can feel soft moss beneath my paws. I feel like I'm going to choke if I get careless and breathe in the mist.

I wonder if this water feeds into the brook where we rested.

"Woof. *(Garo said the nest was behind the waterfall.)*"

It looks like we can get behind the waterfall if we go around the side.

I quickly lead the way, minding the slippery boulders.

We draw closer until the waterfall is right in front of us, but the sound of rushing water is so loud, I feel like my eardrums are going to burst.

I lean against a wall of boulders so I don't get washed away as we inch closer.

"So it's in here…"

Zenobia mumbles as she pulls up her drenched hair.

The humongous waterfall is now behind us. In front is the entrance to a massive cave.

Summer may have just begun, but the cold air blowing from within the cave gives me a chill.

"Let's go."

"Arf. *(Remember, Zenobia. We're going to get the plant and then run for it. We have to avoid a confrontation at all costs.)*"

If worse comes to worst, at the very least, please protect me. Please!

"Hey, let's get a move on. You're leading us in."

"Arw. *(Ohhh, of course. I'm in front…)*"

If we encounter the dragon, I'm seriously running for it.

You can handle the rest, Zenobia.

† † †

"This place is huge…"

The cave is so massive that even her murmur echoes.

Stalactites that could be taller than the mansion hang down from the ceiling.

How huge must this dragon be to live in a cave this large?

We continue into the cavern, afraid that the dragon is in here somewhere, but I can't sense anything.

I can't even smell anything out of the ordinary.

I can't sense any danger, but I also can't find what we came for.

The worst possible thing would be to find out that the dragon was just a legend and there's no wyrmnil here at all.

We would have come all this way for nothing.

I don't want to encounter a dragon, but I really hope it lives here. I hope it just stepped out and we're here alone. Then we can just grab the plant and go. I wouldn't mind that at all.

"Come on, dragon. Where are you hiding?"

Zenobia grumbles, her hand on the hilt of her sword.

"Arf?! *(Zenobia?! That's not what we came here for!)*"

Why does this woman constantly want to fight?!

Our goal is a plant, not a fight!

I feel uneasy as I look back deep into the cave and continue walking.

It's as dark in the cave as it was in the forest, but that didn't matter for those of us with great night vision. We continue through the pitch-black darkness when I spot something faint shining deeper in the cave.

"Arf?! *(Is that it?!)*"

I can smell something sweet like flowers. I hurry toward the light and scent. The path splits into two, but I follow the glowing one without a second thought.

"H-hold up—not so fast."

Zenobia follows a little behind me until we arrive at the glowing spot.

"This is…!"

"Woof, woof! *(Wh-whooooaaaa!)*"

The part of the cave we stop in glows a green phosphorescent color.

Flowers that look like lily of the valley grow in abundance along the cave floor. Their stalks and leaves are transparent, and each dangling flower emits a faint glow. They look like glass sculptures.

We stare a little while at this fantastical sight.

"So this is wyrmnil…?"

"Arf… *(Most likely…)*"

There's nothing else plantlike growing in this place, so that settles it.

We don't know how much we need, so we just stuff as much as we can into the bag Zenobia brought with her.

"Right. This should be enough…"

"Woof, woof… *(If we're done, then let's get out of here…)*"

Zenobia stands up, her bag filled to the brim with wyrmnil.

I don't want to stay here any longer than we have to. We need to get these back to Hecate so she can make some medicine for Lady Mary.

We leave the cave of wyrmnil and head back to the path we followed in.

And that's when it appears.

There before us, more imposing than I could have ever imagined, was the blue dragon.

"GROOOUUUUUUUUUU…"

Its low cry shakes the cave.

It's huge. How could it be this huge?

It's so immense, its head scrapes the ceiling of the cave.

The scales covering its body are sharp and shine like armor, and its limbs look as sturdy as tree trunks.

How long has this thing lived?

Four horns branch off its head, stretching out like a crown.

"GROOOAAAR…"

Its breath is so hot it turns to steam.

Its pupils are straight black slits through yellow irises, and they're looking right at us.

I cannot fathom what those cold eyes are feeling right now.

It's looking down on us like a lord looks down at stones on the roadside.

Our ranks on the food chain are way too different.

"Woof! *(Welp!)*"

My expression tightens as I look the dragon right in the eyes and wet myself.

All over the floor.

Dear Lady Mary.

This is your beloved pet, Routa.

I successfully managed to find the wyrmnil, but it looks like it will take a while to get it back to you. I swear I will return with it, so please wait just a little longer.

If I include my time in the other world, I'll be hitting thirty soon, but I just sprang a massive leak.

I'm embarrassed to say it came out full throttle.

Everything is being expelled from my bladder.

Yep, there it goes.

My paws are completely soaked.

Ahhhhhh! How embarrassing! This is just too embarrassing!

Wetting myself at thirty is so embarrassing!

"... *(Glare.)*"

I have to trick it as I put on a face and look up at the dragon, but internally, I'm writhing with agony.

Ahhh! This is the worst!

I'm positive Zenobia's noticed, too!

Still peeing. Everywhere.

I'm stuck like this; I just can't make it stop!

"GOOAAAAAAAAA!!"

The dragon towering before me lets out a roar.

The air ripples, and a few stalactites break and fall.

This is bad. It's really mad.

"Hufuuuu…"

The dragon, covered in metallic, pale-blue scales, lets out a long breath and lowers its head.

I'm so scared I can't move.

And if I moved now, I'd step in my own pee.

"GORRUOO… *(Entering someone's nest without permission and trying to mark your territory… You are a bold one, aren't you…?)*"

Crap. I've done something really offensive.

I just noticed that I can understand what this dragon's saying. It's just like with Garo and the other wolves. I can hear what's being said over the growls.

"Huff…"

The dragon's face is now so close that I can feel its hot breath. Zenobia doesn't breathe.

I can hear her teeth chattering. Even she can't hide how afraid she is of this dragon.

I know how you feel. All four of my legs are shaking.

She hasn't wet herself yet, so she's doing better than I am. I'm already past my limit.

Do what you must, oh body of mine.

You could say we're like frogs frozen in a serpent's gaze, but the serpent is a dragon.

This is going to end with us getting trampled flat.

"GARRROOOOO…! *(Ha-ha, gya-ha-ha-ha! You're interesting. You're a brave one to do that in front of me. You have piqued my interest. Let us enjoy some tea and treats.)*"

The dragon is clearly smiling.

Its face isn't smiling, but I can tell there's no malice in its voice.

Huh? So it's not mad at us?

We broke into its home and even peed on its floor; I would have thought it would be livid.

Is this dragon actually really friendly?

I instantly lose all fear that my life is in danger. And my urine stream finally stops.

I look up at the dragon's face again. It's a lot less terrifying now that it's so close. Even though it's big enough to swallow someone like me whole.

"GURRROOOOO… *(You came with this female human. I do not have guests in my nest all that often. I am the blue dragon Lenowyrm. I hope you will enjoy my hospitalities.)*"

Ohhh, it looks like this will all be resolved peacefully.

Thank goodness. Fighting this dragon would be a stupid thing to do.

Better than being treated as a snack.

Just as I've calmed down and am about to reply to the dragon—

"R-run for it…"

—I'm interrupted by Zenobia's shaking voice.

"Woof. *(Ah, crap.)*"

Zenobia can't understand what the dragon's saying.

I go back over what just happened, taking out the dragon's voice over its growl.

It roared so loud that the cave shook, then slowly lowered its face toward us while growling.

Yeah, it would look like it was saying, "I'm going to eat you."

"Woof, woof! *(Zenobia, stop! Stay! Staaay!)*"

"Take this and run. I'll sacrifice myself to kill it!"

My frantic barking is all for naught as she takes off the bag with the wyrmnil, throws it at me, then retrieves the sword from her back.

"Haaaaaaaah!!"

She grips the hilt and gets fired up. Something similar to black smoke starts rising from the blade.

"GAROOOOO… *(Wh-what are you doing? Why are you brandishing your sword? Don't you like tea? I have sweets, too…)*"

That's not it, dragon. She just doesn't understand you. Please realize this.

"Go! Routa! You have to get out! Get back to the lady!"

Why does this have to be the first time she calls me by my name...?!

I'm happy, but I'm also not!

Zenobia! I get that you're willing to sacrifice yourself, but now is not the time!

Sorry for raining on your parade, but knock it off!

You're just going to drag us into a pointless fight!

But I'm not a human, and my words don't reach her. She wields her giant sword and strikes at the dragon's wincing face.

"Arf! *(Please let this sword be a fake, too! Please say it's a mistake! We're in huge trouble if it's not! Ah, come on! Snap! Snap!)*"

I pray this sword will break like the previous ones did every time they hit me. With all my might, I envision the dragon's hard scales shattering Zenobia's giant sword.

My hopes are—crushed.

Scales and flesh tear as the sound of a terrifying attack rings out.

"GUGYAAAAAAAAAAAA?!"

It wooooooooorked?!

Why did it have to be real *this* time?! Why couldn't her ancestors have slipped up and handed a fake heirloom down through the generations?!

The dragon takes a tremendous amount of damage as its hard scales tear under the ruthless attack.

"GUROOOOOOOOOO!!! *(O-owwwwwwwww!!!)*"

A copious amount of blood spills from its face as it leans back.

"GURRROOO...?! *(Wh-why? Why do you attack me...?!)*"

Because your words aren't getting through!

"Woof! Woof! *(Hey, you! Can't you speak human?! She doesn't understand you! Tell her that you don't want to fight!)*"

My legs are frozen solid. I can't move at all!

You can do it, dragon! Do it for me!

"GARORO?! *(What?! Oh dear! I haven't spoken with a human in so long, I forgot to speak her language! I can, though! I can speak human!)*"

"Woof! *(Good! Then explain it to her!)*"

"Um, *eg hef ekki ovin! Vio sukarufm fa meo!*"

"Woof?! *(What the hell was that?!)*"

Can't you speak human at all?! Where is that language even from?!

"Chanting a spell?! I won't let you!!"

Zenobia's nervousness must have melted away with her effective first attack. Now she boldly slices at the dragon's legs.

"GAROOO!! *(Ow! Wh-why?! Is this not the language your people speak?! I'm sure it was the same one I used a thousand years ago!)*"

Of course a one-thousand-year-old language won't wooooooork!!!

The language of a country changes whenever its rulership changes, and only in special cases does a country's language stay the same after one thousand years.

A dragon's sense of time is terrifying.

"If I keep pushing, I'll be able to kill it!"

The aura emitting from Zenobia's giant sword is getting stronger and stronger. The sharp killing blows are wounding the beast.

"GUROOOOOO! *(O-ow! S-stop! Hey! That hurts! You! …Th-that's enough…!)*"

As the dragon is cut, its pain increases until I hear its patience finally give out. Then it snaps.

"GAROOOOOOOOOOOOOO!! *(That's enoooooooouuuuuu-uugh!!)*"

Zenobia's sent flying by the pressure of the wind caused by the dragon unfurling its wings.

"Gya?!"

She doesn't have a moment to stop it. She flies past me, and her back crashes into the wall of the cave; then, she slowly slips down.

The giant sword slips out of her hand, and she lies unmoving among the rubble.

She's completely unconscious.

"Arwf?! *(No way! With just one hit?!)*"

"GAAAAAARUOOOOOO!! *(I will forgive thievery! I will*

forgive urine! But I will not forgive multiple attacks against my person when I am being perfectly civil! Prepare to be punished!!!)"

I am as completely stunned as the dragon behind me is completely furious.

It's clear that Zenobia was at fault, and what the dragon says is absolutely true. She couldn't understand the dragon but nevertheless walked all over its generosity. It'll probably eat her. Zenobia's terrible luck has reached its peak.

"Woof... *(I say that, but I still can't leave her...)*"

I feel like I can finally move again, and I step in front of the dragon to protect the unconscious Zenobia.

"GAROOOOO... *(Move. I have no quarrel with you. I am merely going to punish this woman.)*"

The dragon's eyes are bloodshot with rage, and its breathing is ragged.

It's enraged.

"Woof, woof? *(Look, I'm not saying I don't want to do the same myself, and there's a lot going on here... But how much do you plan on punishing her?)*"

"GUROOOO... *(Until she learns her lesson. I shall inflict as much damage on her as she has done to me.)*"

A human like Zenobia would be ripped apart if she received attacks as bad as those left by that giant sword.

"Woof, woof. *(But she's already unconscious. Surely we can call it even and you can let us go now...)*"

"GAROOOOO...... *(I shall not allow it. I will not allow my maiden body to be harmed like this while the aggressor walks away unpunished.)*"

Wait, you're female?

And did you just call yourself a maiden...?

"Woof, woof! *(Please! Let this slide!)*"

"GAROOOO... *(I already told you no. Unless you wish to be punished as well, move.)*"

"Bark! Bark! *(I'll do something about her! So please!)*"

"GUROOOOOO… *(You are persistent! I have no qualms with you! Now move aside!)*"

"Woof, woof! *(Please reconsider! Please reconsider! Please be leeeeeeeenient!!)*"

GRRRRWWWWWWWWWWWWWWL!!

Whoops, my beam came out.

My desperate plea turned into the white beam of light that comes out of my mouth.

The unintended attack is aimed directly at the dragon's face.

"GURRO!!! *(Watch it!!!)*"

Just before the beam hits, something like a magical barrier appears in front of the dragon and deflects it. The beam shoots off at an angle and blasts through the cave wall to the outside.

"GAROOOO! *(Using ultimate destruction magic right from the start?! That would have killed someone other than myself!)*"

The true nature of the beam has been revealed at an unexpected moment.

So that was magic. Sorry, but it's not exactly helpful information.

More importantly, it seems my efforts at persuading the dragon to back off are back to square one.

This is bad.

"GAROOOOOOOOO!! *(That is how you reply when I said I would spare you?! You are as guilty as the human! I shall devour you both!)*"

The dragon takes a deep breath, and several magical circles appear around her mouth.

"GAROOOOOOOOOOOOOOOOOOON!!"

A spiraling blue flame streaks toward Zenobia and myself.

"GRRRRRRRRWWWWWWWWWL!! *(I DON'T WANNA DIIIIIIIIIIIIE!!)*"

I return a howl beam that cancels out the blue flame.

"GAROOOO… *(To think there is a destructive magic even stronger than my own…! You're a dangerous one! That flame would have reduced mountains to a lake of lava!)*"

"Woof, woof! *(Y-you're the dangerous one here, blowing people away! Did you want to kill us?!)*"

"GARO! *(You're the one who tried to kill me first!)*"

"Woof! Woof! *(Shut up! You thousand-year-old shut-in! Stop whining about being hurt!)*"

"GARO! *(Wh-wh-wh-wh-who are you calling a shut-in?! I go outside! At least once every hundred years to let my scales dry…)*"

"Woof, woof! *(You're a hard-core shut-in! Keep this up, and you're going to start growing moss! You thousand-year-old spinster!)*"

"GAROOOOOO! *(Wh-wh-why did you have to say that?! Spinster is a most terrible insult to call someone! How dare you! How dare you! I won't forgive yoooouuuu!)*"

Our tumultuous bickering overlaps as we exchange beam and blaze.

The flame melts boulders, and the light blows open another hole.

The aftershock of our attacks makes the cave crumble.

"*Wheeze…wheeze…*"

"*Gafooo… Gafoooo…*"

We both run out of breath at the same time and glare at each other, exhausted.

"GAROO… *(Wh-why do you do so much to protect a human maiden such as that…? You are clearly a Fen Wolf, are you not? One thousand years ago, your kind would do terrible things to the humans. Furthermore, this would have never happened if that woman had not started this fight. Why don't you rid yourself of such a terrible human…?)*"

The tired blue dragon Lenowyrm makes a convincing argument.

"Woof, woof… *(…You're probably right. Zenobia's normally got it in for me. Actually, she's already tried to kill me twice. And she probably won't learn from me saving her and will likely try to kill me again.)*"

She is a complete and utter meathead.

"GUROO… *(Then why…?)*"

"Woof, woof… *(Yeah, I'm wondering that, too. She's probably going to get really frustrated and cry when she wakes up and finds out*

I've saved her. She'll say, 'Why you?' and 'I'm so pathetic being saved by a monster.')"

I can easily see her breaking down and crying.

"Woof! *(I really want to lick Zenobia's crying face with her tears and snot mixed together. That's enough reason for me to save her!)*"

My expression is completely serious as I announce this.

"............"

"............"

A slight breeze blows in from the hole in the cave.

"GA, GAROOOOOOOOOOOOOOOOOOOON!! *(P-PER-VEEEEEEEEERRRRRRRRT!!)*"

"GRWWWWWWWWWWWWWL!! *(SHUT UUUUUUU-UUUUUUP!! DON'T UNDERESTIMATE A LICK-A-HOLIIIIIII-IIIIIIIIIIIIIIIIIIC!!)*"

We both voice our strongest roars yet in a terrible flash and a thunderous tumult, which clash together until my whole vision turns white.

The final, blinding white light and blue inferno swell when they meet; then the energy disperses.

The aftershock carves into the cave, burning it away to nothing until the entire place is destroyed.

The violent torrent of magic emits a blinding ivory radiance that forces my eyes closed.

Then, the light slowly begins to fade, and when silence returns to the cave, I open my eyes. There before me is the dragon covered in black smoke.

Its giant body is curled up into a ball like a great black boulder.

"GUROOO… *(I lost…)*"

The earth rumbles, and the blue dragon Lenowyrm collapses.

The wound-covered dragon feebly opens her mouth.

"GAROOO… *(I never thought the day would come when I would lose…and to a pervert, no less.)*"

Don't call me a pervert.

It's in a dog's nature to want to lick things.

"GUROO… *(Well, I certainly have lived a long life…)*"

She lowers herself onto the ground and quietly closes her eyes.

"GUROO… *(I am satisfied. Now you may finish me off…)*"

"Woof. *(No way. Sorry for killing the mood, but I'm not gonna murder you, okay?)*"

This whole fight started from a misunderstanding, after all.

So Lenowyrm was it? It doesn't look like she wants to fight anymore, so there's no point in continuing it any further.

"GAROOO… *(You are sparing my life? Do you not desire the honor of being a dragon slayer?)*"

"Woof. *(I don't know anything about that. What's a pet gonna do with something like that anyway?)*"

What I want is to spend my days eating, sleeping, and getting spoiled rotten. I don't care about anything beyond that.

How many times do I have to say this? Pet life is the best life.

"GAROOO… *(You are not just brave but also compassionate and humble. I shall no longer call you a pervert but a fine creature…)*"

I feel like I'm getting hit on by this thousand-year-old spinster dragon.

But I'm not a furry, so I'm not happy about that at all.

Also, don't call me a pervert.

Anyway, I hope her injuries are all right. She's covered in cuts and burns. It looks really bad.

"GUROOOO… *(Hmph. This is nothing out of the ordinary. These wounds shall heal on their own once I have rested. I very much enjoyed our battle.)*"

"Woof, woof. *(I'm not planning on doing that again, but I suppose you've been all alone in this miserable place for a while. We should hang out next time.)*"

It was easy to tell just from talking to her. Lenowyrm's not a bad dragon at all.

We caused her a lot of problems, so maybe next time I'll bring her some of old man James's cooking as a gift.

"GAROOO… *(You are mean to call it a miserable place. You are at least half responsible for destroying my nest.)*"

"Bark. *(…Yeah, sorry about that.)*"

"GAROOO… *(Ha-ha-ha, I am joking. I am going to sleep now. Feel free to take whatever you like from here. The would-be dragon slayer deserves a fitting prize, after all.)*"

With that, Lenowyrm curls up and closes her eyes.

"Bark. *(Later then, Lenowyrm. I hope we meet again soon.)*"

She waves her giant tail in response.

I laugh at how much that lazy gesture reminds me of myself. Then, I go to wake Zenobia.

† † †

"Arww, arww. *(Zenobia, wake up. It's licking time.)*"

I poke her shoulder with my nose, but she doesn't stir at all.

I already found the bag with the wyrmnil, so now all I have to do is wake Zenobia up and go back home.

"Arww, arww. *(You're not going to like me licking your face. Though I'd rather lick your face when you wake up crying. Wakey, wakey and let me lick you.)*"

"Mewl… *(Oh, Routa, you do have some wicked inclinations…)*"

I suddenly hear a cat behind me.

I'm so surprised, I jump.

"Arwf?! *(Wha—?! N-Nahura?!)*"

"Mewl. *(Yes, it is I, Nahura. My mistress told me that you should be done about now, and so I have come to get you.)*"

It looks like she was there from the start as she climbs up and sits on my back.

She ignores my surprised expression and calmly cleans her face.

"Woof, woof?! *(By 'come to get us,' do you mean chase us out?!)*"

"Mewww. *(Oh, no, not at all. You cannot possibly make it back on foot. We will use a type of spatial magic. Using you as an anchor to fly through space…meow.)*"

Magic's amazing. Who would have thought you can travel some-where in an instant?

Also, her added "meow" to the end of the sentence still feels forced.

"Woof, woof. *(Nahura, you really are an amazing cat.)*"

"Mewl. *(Why, thank you. My magic is limited to three coordinates, though. Mistress's workshop, Gandolf's house, and you.)*"

Me?

So you can mark individuals with it?

"Bark…? *(…You didn't get my permission for that, did you…?)*"

Doesn't that mean she could appear in front of me anywhere, at any time?

Even a pet needs privacy!

"Mewl! *(It was mistress's orders… Please forgive meow!)*"

She lifts her paw in front of her face and waves it like one of those lucky cat statues.

You're soooo cuuuute. I forgiiiive yoooou.

Damn it. You're a tricky one, Nahura.

"Mew. *(Well then, shall we return? I would prefer we leave before we wake up the scary dragon sleeping over there.)*"

"GARROOO… *(I can hear you…)*"

"Mew! *(Waah! Let's go now! Chop-chop!)*"

Nahura starts at Lenowyrm's sleepy voice and leaps onto Zeno-bia's lap.

"Meow. *(Time to move. I hope you haven't forgotten anything.)*"

A white light expands from her body. I wonder if everything within the light will get instantly transported.

I have the bag. I'd rather leave the sword, but unfortunately, it's right next to Zenobia.

"Meeeeooooow!"

Nahura lets out a high-pitched meow, and the scenery warps like haze on a hot day.

A moment later and we're no longer in the dark cave but the large garden of the mansion.

I can see the familiar garden, the large trees, the sparkling fountain.

The home I know all too well.

"Woof… *(It really did only take a moment…)*"

The sun had already risen high into the sky while we were fighting. The sunlight is really bright, though it's probably because I was in that dark cave mere moments ago.

"Welcome back. I see it went well."

Hecate the witch is waiting for us, holding the wide brim of her hat.

"Woof, woof? *(Is this the wyrmnil? Is there enough?)*"

"It is indeed, and you have plenty."

I hand over the bag brimming with wyrmnil.

"I shall begin refining the medicine immediately. Nahura, could you please examine Zenobia?"

"Mew. *(Yes! I understand, meow.)*"

"Woof, woof. *(Thank you, Hecate.)*"

"Leave it to me."

I watch Hecate gracefully leave, then I dash to my lady's room.

Sorry, Zenobia, but I'll have to lick your crying face another time.

I sprint down the corridor, past a maid (she angrily shouts that I shouldn't run inside), and don't stop until I get to her room.

"Woof! Woof! *(My lady! I got you medicine! You'll be better in no time!)*"

I use my front paws to open the door and dart inside.

"Oh my, Routa. Wherever did you get to? The young lady was so worried about you."

The maid Miranda stands up from her chair.

She must have been watching over Lady Mary this whole time. There are bags under her eyes.

"Woof! *(I'm sorry!)*"

I apologize to her and then put my front paws up on the bed to peek at my lady's face.

"…Routa?"

She opens her eyes, the fever still apparent.

"Routa…!"

She soon gets teary.

"Where did you go…? You weren't here… I was so worried…!"

She wraps her arms around my neck and pushes her face into me.

Her body is so hot, it feels like it's on fire.

It looks like it's time for some of Hecate's fever medicine.

She looks exhausted.

It breaks my heart to have left her in a state where after only half a day she's already this lonely.

"Arww, arww. *(I'm sorry, my lady. But I had to get medicine to make you better.)*"

"Routa… Routa… Don't leave me again……"

"Arww. *(I won't. I promise I won't go anywhere.)*"

I remain in her embrace until Hecate's medicine is delivered.

† † †

After drinking the more effective medicine, Lady Mary's fever immediately goes down.

When she wakes up that evening, Papa cries and rubs his cheek against hers.

"Ahhhh!!! Maaaaaryyyy! Thank goodness! Thank goooooooodness!"

"Ohhh, Father, your beard tickles."

She gently hugs her father as he clings to her.

"Lady Mary!"

That's when Zenobia bursts in.

Looks like she's awake, too.

I don't know if Nahura treated her or not, but her wounds from her fight with Lenowyrm appear healed.

"Oh, Zenobia."

Lady Mary smiles at her arrival.

"Miss, your illness…?!"

"Yes, I'm completely better. I heard you went to get the ingredients for the medicine for me. Thank you."

"Zenobia! Please allow me to give you my thanks! Thank you so much!"

Sweat and tears stream down Papa's face as he shakes her hand.

"I had heard about this ingredient when I was looking for various treatments. Wyrmnil is a mystical medicinal plant that only grows in a dragon's nest. You went into a very dangerous place and even fought a dragon for Mary's sake, right?"

"Huh?! No, I…!"

Zenobia is bewildered at Papa's effusive praise.

"I saw a beam of light in the sky far off in the distance the other night. It must have been a fierce battle. I'm certain that was you. Who else could it have been but an SS Rank Adventurer? I'm glad you came into our home. I must give you something to thank you! Just tell me—anything!"

"No! That wasn't me! I couldn't do anything…"

Zenobia thinks this is all a big misunderstanding.

But when you look at it, the only one who could have fought a dragon was Zenobia.

She lost consciousness at the end, and when she awoke, she was back in the mansion. Now everyone's treating her like a hero.

Thus her confusion.

"No…? But the wyrmnil… If it wasn't you…then who…?"

This time it's Papa's turn to be bewildered at her adamant denial.

Yesterday, the only ones not in the mansion were Zenobia and one other.

In other words: me.

Everyone's gaze turns toward me.

"Arw! *(…Ah!)*"

C-craaaap!

I was so preoccupied with getting the wyrmnil that I didn't think about what came after.

Hecate, who normally follows me around, isn't here.

Anyone watching from a distance could tell someone was fighting a dragon at that moment in time.

Everyone must think it's strange that an ordinary dog could fight a dragon.

Now my real identity will be discovered.

"Routa…?"

Miranda the maid looks down at me with fearful eyes.

"Arww, arww! *(You've got it wrong, Miranda! I'm just a cute widdle puppy! Don't look at me like that! Really! Please! Please don't take this life away from meeeee…!)*"

I move to cling to her, but she takes a step back.

Uwah, that hurts…!

"Routa, you didn't…?"

Even Papa asks me with a trembling voice.

C-crap. Now even Papa, the head of the house, suspects me…!

What do I do…?! What do I do…?!

Oh no, I need to think of something…!

"It can't be… Did Routa really…?"

"—Haaa! Ha-ha-ha!!"

A lighthearted laugh breaks the silence.

"I guess I've been found out! That's right. I was the one who defeated the dragon and returned with the wyrmnil! It was a formidable foe but, well, you can see how that went!"

Zenobia puffs out her chest as she boasts.

"Arw…? *(You're going to help me just in the nick of time…?)*"

She's a terrible ham of an actor.

Judging from her personality, she must hate taking credit for such a feat.

And now she has to put on this performance all…for my sake?

"Ohhh, so it was you! You really are amazing, Zenobia!"

"Ha! Ha! Ha! Ha! Not at all! Routa here wasn't helpful at all. I took him along, but he couldn't do anything. He was scared the whole time! He really is just an ordinary dog! Ha! Ha! Ha! Ha!"

So she's going to help me hide my real identity.

Though you can tell she hates the lie from the way she grips her shaking hands.

Forgive me. Forgive me, Zenobia.

Please hold out just a little longer, for my sake…!

Everyone continues praising Zenobia and saying how *amaaaaazing* she is for a good while after that.

† † †

"Gromff omff! *(Delicious! So good! The old man's food really is the best!)*"

I greedily devour the first piece of cured boar steak that's been seasoned with salt and grilled to perfection.

It's a thick cut of meat that was cooked in the oven on the lowest heat, then seared over a high flame, making the outside crisp but the inside nice and rare. As it's cooked all the way through, there's no smell, but its juiciness remains. The meat overflows with umami-rich juices when I bite into it.

So, so, sooo good! This is the work of a master chef!

"Mewww! *(It really is delicious! Routa!)*"

"Woof, woof! *(Yeah! It's the best! Hey, Nahura, can you stop sneaking bites of my dinner?)*"

That's mine! Go get Hecate to make some for you!

"Mew. *(Aw, don't be so stingy. Let me have half. Only half. ♪)*"

"Woof, woof! *(You're going to eat half of this?! Your cheekiness is shocking!)*"

I don't care how cutely you say it. I won't forgive you!

"Squeak, squeak. *(Indeed. Understand your place, insolent cat.)*"

Squeak?

I feel like I heard a strange voice just now.

"Squeak, squeak. *(Mmm, but it is indeed as you said. This meat is simply divine. Very good. You should bring me more.)*"

I look down at my plate to see a small mouse sitting on the edge.

It's using both its paws skillfully to nibble on a piece of meat.

Its fur is a unique color, a fresh blue.

"Mewww! *(A-a mouse?! I hate mice! Kill it, Routa! Get it!)*"

Nahura lets out a scream.

"Arwf... *(You're a cat that's scared of mice... You're certainly an odd one...)*"

"Squeak. *(You really are so noisy. It is I.)*"

The blue mouse runs up my leg and onto my head.

"Arwf. *(H-hey.)*"

"Squeak. *(What? You were the one who said I should visit. And so I have come all this way. Should you not be more welcoming?)*"

This brazen way of speaking, I feel like I've heard it somewhere before.

"Bark! *(It can't be! Lenowyrm?!)*"

"Squeak, squeak. *(Indeed. You've finally realized. My original form would be most terrifying for humans. And so I came in one that would not stand out. I am, after all, a polite maiden who knows the appropriate manners for any time and place.)*"

She did demonstrate those manners when we met.

Wait, so she can transform at will?

Perhaps the reason there aren't many sightings of dragons is because they've transformed and are living lives as other creatures...?

Whoa.

I think I may have discovered one of this world's secrets.

That's too much knowledge for a simple dog. Let's just forget about it.

"Squeak, squeak. *(So there you have it. I shall board here for now.)*"

"Arwf?! *(What?! Why?! Aren't you going home?!)*"

"Squeak? *(Who was it that destroyed my nest?)*"

"...Arww... *(Me...)*"

"Squeak. *(Hmph. As long as you understand that. Hmm, your fur is most comfortable to sleep in. It's decided. I shall make this my new nest!)*"

Her nest? She's going to live in my fur?!

But I did destroy her home, so I'm not in any position to argue.

It's like getting a tick...

"Squeak. *(And so, I have judged you, the one who defeated me, as satisfactory. I am a little concerned that you are a pervert, but love is blind. You should be grateful I have decided to make you my groom.)*"

This no-good mouse sure is saying some ridiculous stuff.

My reply is immediate.

"Bark. *(No way.)*"

"Squeak! *(Wh-what did you say?! I'll have you know, ruffian, that I am one of the most beautiful among all dragons!)*"

"Woof, woof! *(I already said, I'm not a fuuuuurryyyyy!!)*"

I bark angrily at the blue mouse that just shrieked in my ear.

"Mewww. *(Oh yes. This meat really is fantastic.)*"

I look over to Nahura, who clearly isn't listening, and see my plate is now empty.

"Woof! *(H-how dare you eat someone's food the moment they step away!)*"

"Squeak! *(What a terrible greedy cat! You have really done it now!)*"

"Woof! Woof! *(Nahura! Let me tell you something! There is nothing more terrifying than my grudge for eating my fooooooood! You! Give me back my meeeeaaaat!!)*"

"M-myaaa?! *(N-noooooooo?!)*"

And so, a terribly long companionship between a no-good dog, a useless cat, and a hopeless mouse begins.

Epilogue

It's been a week since we brought the wyrmnil back. The medicine worked perfectly, and my lady is already back to full health. The frantic mansion returns to normal, and I continue my life as a pampered pooch.

I've enjoyed the usual five-star meal prepared by the old man, and now I'm napping in the shade of a tree.

There's this strange, uncomfortable feeling, but that may be due to my two new houseguests.

I now have a blue mouse living on my back, and a crimson cat is lying on a tree branch above my head.

I'm just going to ignore them. They're not going to leave even if I tell them to.

Now that my lady's illness is gone, she sticks to me like glue. Even now, she's sleeping soundly with her arms around me.

Oh man, it's hard being so popular. Guess I've used up my pet luck.

"Hey, this makes us even."

I suddenly hear Zenobia's voice coming from behind the tree.

"I don't know what happened when I fainted, but that was all your doing, right?"

I don't answer her.

Because I'm just a simple pet dog.

"Honestly, you forced me to make such a big deal over it. I've never been so embarrassed in all my life. And yet, I do owe you one. I could not have done it by myself. Thank you for saving the young lady."

Wow. Zenobia just thanked me.

The sky isn't gonna fall tomorrow, is it?

"But don't get me wrong. I still don't trust you. I will cut you down the day you return to your monster ways."

She warns me, then walks off.

You need to be more honest with yourself.

The urge to lick grows ever stronger.

"Arwf… *(The weather really is nice today…)*"

The rays of the early summer sun are getting stronger, but the shade of the tree is still cool.

I decide to have a bit of a nap and lay my head on my front paws.

A strong breeze blows by, and my lady opens her eyes.

"Hmm…"

"Woof, woof? *(Oh, you're awake, my lady? You don't have studies for a while longer, so we can relax! Or perhaps we could play fetch?)*"

Her sleepy eyes look back at me before her expression quickly softens, and she puts her arms around me again for a hug.

"Thank goodness you're still here, Routa… I'd hate for you to leave me again."

"Woof, woof. *(I know. Your Routa will always be by your side. I promise.)*"

She looks right into my eyes and smiles. It's like watching a beautiful flower bloom.

"I love you, Routa!"

Yeah. It was all worth it to see this smile.

I'll say it again, and again, and again.

Pet life is the best life!!!

EX — What a Kind Goddess! ...Or So I Thought, but She Was Actually Useless!

"YOUR WISH SHALL BE GRANTED!!!"

My fading consciousness awakens in the darkness to a loud voice.

"Huh?! What the—?!"

I try to collect myself, but I'm still a bit dazed. My nose and lips hurt where I smacked them on the company floor when I collapsed.

They really hurt. My front teeth are broken. I'm sure they are.

"...Huh? Wait a sec. I don't actually feel any pain."

I don't feel anything at all; I also don't have a body.

I try to put my hand on my banged-up face, but it's not there. I'm a spirit floating in midair.

"What is this? What's going on...?"

The pure-white floor below me expands as far as the eye can see, and a blue sky, so vast I feel I could fall into it, spreads out over the horizon.

It's an incredibly beautiful sight, but shouldn't this be the slightly dirty company floor where I dropped dead?

Where in the world am I?

"Routa Okami."

"Yes?"

A voice suddenly calls out to me.

It must be the woman's voice I heard before.

How can I put it? She has an "If you would like to make a deposit, please enter your four-digit PIN number" kind of voice.

I see. She's a scammer.

"Am not."

She refutes as if she just read my mind. At the same time, a ring of blinding light carves a hole in the sky, and someone appears from within. The figure slowly floats down as if possessed of wings. The ring of light shrinks, then hangs above the person's head.

"It is a pleasure to meet you, Routa Okami. I am sure this must be a shock to you, so please allow me to explain what happened."

The smiling woman looks soft and warm. Her hair is soft, her clothes are soft, her expression is soft. She's like an affectionate big sister. She exudes a nurturing aura.

"That is because I am a goddess. I am the mother of all life on earth."

A soft, smiling goddess big sister.

Ugh. If I had a body, this would be when I'd rush forward and hug her, saying "Mama!"

"If that is what you desire, you are more than welcome. Would you like a nice big hug?"

"Oh, um, sorry. I'm not brave enough for that... Wait, goddess?!"

"Yes. Or rather, I am a single low-ranking god who has finally been assigned souls to take care of."

"Ohhh... You're different from what I had imagined."

I had envisioned some wizened old fogy with a white beard and a scary face.

"Some of my superiors look like that. But they say that the most important thing is to show dignity, otherwise humans will start to disrespect you."

Sorry, but that's exactly how I feel right now. I never thought God would be a soft, mature woman with a full chest.

So the gods' society is ruled by hierarchies, too. I can't say if that's efficient or messed up.

And I feel like she's been reading my thoughts for a while now.

"Well, I *am* a goddess."

Please stop reading my thoughts! That's a breach of privacy!

"I am joking. It's written all over your face. You are a very honest person, Routa."

I don't have a face. I'm just a floating soul here.

"Now that you seem to have calmed down, I shall explain the situation to you."

"Oh. Okay."

Seems like that was just a pep talk to get me to relax. But considering this space apart from reality, a woman who says she's a god, and myself being a spirit-like thing…I have a pretty good idea of what happened.

"Routa Okami, you are dead."

"Ahh, I knew it. I thought so…"

I knew that had happened, so it wasn't as much of a shock as I thought it'd be.

So I did die back then.

I don't have any regrets about dying.

I only have distant relatives, so I wonder what they'll do about my funeral and savings.

I just wish someone would take the chance to dispose of my smartphone and computer as well as a few select items in my room.

Please sympathize with me. Boss, you're my only hope. As the only person who ever talked to me, a nerd like you must surely empathize with someone like me who has no friends. Just go in there with a hammer and drill and destroy all my stuff before they take it away.

"Oh yes. It would be nice if someone would destroy those things before any embarrassing information was leaked."

"Can you really read that from my face?"

You're really reading my mind, aren't you?!

"No, no, your face looked like it was pleading for someone to destroy some evidence."

What does that even mean? I don't even have a face.

"Oh yes, about that. As you have died, we would normally have you return to the cycle of death and rebirth, but right now, we are holding a special promotion."

Promotion. That sounds very earthlike. Heaven is just like earth.

"Well, you see, in recent years, we have had a lot of people who have refused to return to the cycle of death and rebirth. Previously, everyone wanted to be reborn because they did not want to die, but now, so many people would rather vanish than live another hard life."

Yeah, I know how they feel. I hate the idea of becoming a corporate slave again.

So there are loads more unhappy people in the world besides me? Does anyone have a strong enough desire to keep living?

I don't care about that! My misfortune will decide for me!

I don't want to work! I never want to work ever again!

"There are a lot of people who think like that."

"You really are reading my mind, aren't you?! Aren't you?!"

"Oh, no, it shows on your face."

I don't have a face.

"So about our promotion. If you cannot bear the reality of this world, then perhaps you would like to try being reincarnated in a different world. We've only just begun this promotion, but there have been a lot of people taking this option."

I get it. I understand that. I understand being influenced by pop culture at a young age all too well.

This is "being reborn in another world."

"Thank goodness you caught on fast."

"You're reading my min—"

"—Your face."

Let's just get back on topic.

"Very well, Routa Okami. I heard your wish for rebirth when you died. You want to be a dog, correct?"

"Yes!"

"All right, then. Let me make some preparations...... Huh? A dog? Like a puppy?"

"Yes!"

A dog! A dog belonging to a rich family! The type of dog who's soft and flabby and gets fed lots of fattening food!

"Wh-what a strange request... A lot of humans ask to be reborn as different creatures, but it seems that most of them are close relatives to humans."

I'm guessing things like elves and vampires. I can understand why some people would want to be reborn as a fantastical being. They're being reborn in another world. They probably want to be beautiful or get a bunch of cheater abilities to take with them.

"But I want to be a dog. A rich family's dog."

I mean, after all, getting reborn as a creature that looks like a human would still come with lots of work, right? And I don't want to have to deal with human interactions, either. I've had enough of that struggle.

I want to spend my days lazing about, not thinking about anything, being spoiled by my owner, and not having my stomach hurt from anxiety over worrying about the next day.

If someone could grant me that, then I'd be happy to be reborn in any world.

"R-really? If that is your wish, then I shall grant it."

Yes! Hell yes!

"Becoming a nonhuman species means your spirit shall also change shape, meaning I have to make a number of adjustments, but you will essentially still be you, with all your memories. You may feel some slight instability until I can place you in a physical body, but your memories and personality should return to you."

"Okay. That sounds fine to me."

I didn't realize how lucky I'd be when I died of overwork. Nothing particularly good happened in my life, so I was never expecting this plot twist at the last second.

Thank you, goddess. Now I can be a happy dog.

"You wish to be reincarnated as a pet dog to rich owners. Is that correct?"

"Yes!"

That's exactly what I want. Nothing more.

Oh, although it would be nice if my owner was a cute girl.

Being the pet of a filthy-rich, hairy, fat guy is a little…

I'm sure I'd live a lavish lifestyle, but I don't imagine being the pet of some gangster would come with much coddling.

"Very well. Just relax and let yourself slip away."

"Understood."

I close my eyes as my chest swells with the desire to pass on to the next world. Not that I have any eyes.

"Everything is in constant flux. This being shall be liberated from his previous world and be reincarnated in the next. The goddess Aphrodite commands it."

She spreads out her arms, and I am bathed in a dazzling light.

It's finally time. I'm kissing my human world good-bye and getting reincarnated as a rich dog.

The pet life I've only ever dreamed of is finally here!

"But you know, I am a little worried about leaving it at that."

"Huh?"

The goddess speaks up *just* as I'm about to be reincarnated.

"What is there to worry about?"

"Well, lots of other people wished for overpowered physical or magical abilities in preparation for the journeys ahead. You won't have anything at all, though, and I don't think that's fair. You are so modest that I feel compelled to grant you a few small boons."

"Huh? Um, goddess…?"

I don't need any boons.

I'm just happy being the dog of a rich family.

"Let's see. Regular dogs only live for about fifteen years. That is rather pitiful. Let's increase your life span."

Okay, that's not so bad.

A few extra days to laze around should be more than enough.

"Let's add an extra thousand years for now."

"Huh?"

A thousand?! Why?! A goddess's idea of standard is way too huge!

"Also, the next world is full of monsters, so it might be quite dangerous. Let's have you be reincarnated into a powerful creature closely related to a dog."

"Huh?"

Closely related to a dog?! I want to be reincarnated as an *actual* dog, though! Not something that just looks like a dog!!!

"Oh, this one looks good. It is a particularly powerful variation called a Fen Wolf. It's the King of the Fen Wolves known as Fenrir. It's a bit big, but since it does look a lot like a dog, it being huge is a trivial matter."

"Huh?"

Goddess?! What are you summoning from that huge book of yours?! What is that catalog?! What's written in there about the recommended reincarnations?! And it being huge is not a trivial matter!

"It comes with a lot of magical powers. Oh, wow. It's the strongest ranking creature here. It's so strong, you can destroy it seven times without killing it."

"Huh?"

Why's it so strong? Wait—that's not the issue here!

"Yes, yes, you would have a difficult time when you get into a fight because you have lived in such a peaceful country. I shall install some half-self-activating offensive magic. One that will destroy a mountain in a single shot. I am sure that you will find some use for such powerful magic."

"Huh?"

That sounds terrifying. That's not what I want! I don't need any of that!

"Oh, no, no need to thank me. It is my job to ensure that your reincarnation goes smoothly, after all."

That's not it! That's not what I want! I'm happy being a simple pampered pooch!

Why do you have to add all these unnecessary features?!

"Well then, have a nice afterlife!"

"Just listen to meeeeeeeeeeeeeeeeeeeeee!!"

Can you see my face telling you to stooooooooooooooopppppp?!

† † †

"Arwf?! *(N-wha—?!)*"

I snap awake.

That was a memory from before I was reincarnated. I was able to remember it clearly in my dream.

"Arww. *(Ohhh…right. That's it. I remember now.)*"

It's all that dumb goddess's fault. It's thanks to all these unnecessary features she gave me that I'm the King of the Fen Wolves.

It's her fault my pet life is a colossal mess.

I never asked to be targeted by a knight, or to have a bunch of Fen Wolves make me do those reckless things, or to have a death battle with a dragon.

"Bark! Bark! *(I won't forget this, you useless goddess…! I'm gonna give you a piece of my mind the next time I die!)*"

I swear to the blue sky above me.

"What's wrong, Routa? Why are you howling at the sky?"

Lady Mary looks up from the book she's reading and strokes my cheek.

"Arww. *(It's nothing. I'm just getting ready to complain to a goddess.)*"

I rub my face against her cheek, and she squints her eyes as it tickles her.

We were having a break in the shade of the large tree in the garden, but I must have dozed off at some point.

She leans against my body and resumes her reading.

Once more, I've taken on the role of the sofa.

"Arwf. *(I suppose I'm thankful that I ended up with my lady somehow.)*"

I'm pretty sure I hit the owner jackpot.

There's no doubt about it. She's the best mistress ever.

"Arwoo! *(But I still won't forgive you for giving me this Fenrir body! I refuse to! I won't forget this, you worthless goddess!!)*"

As I bear this grudge against a goddess who refused to listen to me, I howl at the sky.

† † †

Meanwhile, in the heavenly plane.

A goddess managing the departed souls in the cycle of rebirth is taking a break from work.

"I wonder what Routa is doing right now? He was the one who made that odd request to be turned into a dog."

I gave him a lot of unique features as a special service. I wonder if his life is going well?

The worried goddess decides to take a peek.

She spreads out her arms, and a hole appears in the white floor.

She sees a young girl and a dog snuggling under a large tree.

The dog is so huge and its face so ferocious, you can't really call it a dog anymore, but that's a trivial problem for the goddess.

The human and creature seem incredibly happy.

The dog looks up at her as if he notices he's being watched from the heavens and lets out a wild howl.

The goddess looks at him and chuckles softly.

"Hee-hee, I'm happy you're happy. I hope you enjoy your second life, Routa, or would that be your 'dog life'?"

The dog's howl sounded rather angry, but the goddess just took it as a howl of thanks.

The dog's rage never reaches the goddess. In her mind, she doesn't need to hear words of praise. She gets embarrassed easily, so she's a bit shy.

Afterword

To all my first-time readers, it's a pleasure to meet you.

To those who know me from my very first novel, *Alto Ciel of the Azure*, good morning, good evening, and good night.

Those who have known about me for a while are probably already great friends, so come on in! Make yourself at home! Would you like something to eat? Gwa-ha-ha! (Just like old man James.)

Let me start again. Thank you so much for picking up this book.

This is the official publication of my light novel, which I uploaded to the novel websites *Kakuyomu* and *Shousetsuka ni Narou*.

I'm thankful for the advice of a senior author who told me, "The most important thing for writing a novel is to write what you want." That made it easy to create and release, and from that came everyone's support, until finally this new novel came out. I'm just overflowing with joy.

Of course, it also made me a million times busier. I want a break!

It's been only four months since my debut, and I'm already on my third volume. I want a break!

My schedule was hell. I want a break!

But by focusing my anger on that desire for a vacation, rather than on my editor in chief, I was able to put everything into this novel, *Woof Woof Story: I Told You to Turn Me Into a Pampered Pooch, Not Fenrir!*

Days off. Overtime. Commuting. Not making the last train. Those days of hard work wore me out, and I really wanted some therapy with a cute, fluffy animal. No, I really wanted to become something that would get all the head pats. I wanted a cute master to take care of me, to eat delicious food, to sleep as much as I wanted, to not have to worry about my future, and to take it easy and be spoiled every day.

Let me shake your hand if you feel that way, too. Let's become Routa together.

Now let me thank everyone who helped make this book a reality.

First of all, everyone who read the online version of this story! You supported me with your comments and reviews. Thanks to that, I was able to get the physical version done. Thank you so much! The online version is still ongoing, so I hope you keep enjoying it!

My editor K, who helped me with the third volume of *Woof Woof!* I'm a terrible author who doesn't work if not being hounded, but you really saved me by keeping me to the schedule and somehow making all the deadlines! But, um, could you maybe allow a little more breathing room in the future?

Kochimo, who drew some colorful illustrations that really made the novel pop: the cool yet super-fluffy Fenrir, a kind and energetic young lady, a no-good knight, and a sexy witch. You brought them to life along with a variety of other characters through your fantastic designs. Thank you! I smile every time I look at them!

Also, the artist and author, my teacher, 47AgDragon (Shirudora), who taught me the importance of language in character creation and story structure when I was just writing on instinct.

To everyone at the publishing company, designers, proofreaders, marketers, booksellers—it was thanks to all the people who supported me that this publication happened. Thank you so much!

And of course, my biggest thanks to you, who picked up this book.

Sorry for keeping it short.

I hope to see you again in future volumes! Until then!

2017.9 Inumajin